BETWEEN
CLAY
AND
DUST

MUSHARRAF ALI FAROOQI

BETWEEN CLAY AND DUST

First published in India in 2012 by Aleph Book Company.
This edition published in Canada in 2014 by Freehand Books, an imprint of Broadview Press.
Copyright © Musharraf Ali Farooqi 2012

Freehand Books gratefully acknowledges the support of the Canada Council for the Arts for its publishing program. ◀ Freehand Books, an imprint of Broadview Press Inc., acknowledges the financial support for its publishing program provided by the Government of Canada through the Canada Book Fund.

  Canada Council   Conseil des Arts
for the Arts   du Canada   Government

Freehand Books
515 – 815 1st Street sw   Calgary, Alberta   T2P 1N3
www.freehand-books.com

Book orders: LitDistCo
100 Armstrong Avenue   Georgetown, Ontario   L7G 5S4
Telephone: 1-800-591-6250   Fax: 1-800-591-6251
orders@litdistco.ca   www.litdistco.ca

Library and Archives Canada Cataloguing in Publication
Farooqi, Musharraf, 1968–, author
Between clay and dust / Musharraf Ali Farooqi.
ISBN 978-1-55481-207-3 (pbk.)
I. Title.
PS8611.A76B48 2014   C813'.6   C2014-902293-X

Book design by Natalie Olsen, Kisscut Design
Author photo by Nina Subin

Printed on FSC recycled paper and bound in Canada

This is a work of fiction. Names, characters, places and incidents are either the product of the author's imagination or are used fictitiously and any resemblance to any actual persons, living or dead, events or locales is entirely coincidental.

FOR

Afzal Ahmed Syed

INNER CITY

The ruination of the inner city was attributed to time's proclivity for change. It lay abandoned, half buried in and half surrounded by the squalor of shanty towns. New settlements cordoning it on three sides seemed to avoid the shadow of its sunken grandeur. Streets connecting new colonies skirted off its periphery. Links binding old and new neighbourhoods were either never formed or broken at the start. The wide serpentine alley of high, arched gateways dividing its residential and artisan quarters looked strangely desolate.

The ravaging winds of Partition had left it unscathed. The turmoil that had seared the fibre of men and gored their souls had not touched this quiet habitation. There had been anxiety that things would be greatly changed, but later there seemed hope that the worst was over and life's routines could now be renewed. Nobody expected that in Partition's wake would follow a slow disintegration of values that would unravel the inner city. In a way, the inner city was always a cat's cradle – a crisscross of life's many faces, each sustained by the other. The strings of this cat's cradle had not snapped but they had become hopelessly tangled.

The inner city had been emptied of most of its old inhabitants. Just as its walls had been stripped of their turquoise-coloured mosaic panels, time's ravages had forced into oblivion its generations of the dead, too. To answer the fierce demand for construction material during the last few years, the memory of those who had shaped the inner city was not only stripped of the tombstones that commemorated their existence, but also the bricks that marked their graves.

The disfigured architecture and worn, paved stones of the inner city still intoned its past splendour in broken whispers. There were a few enclaves where the last of its remnants were yet visible. Unconcerned and out of step with the currents of time, even after the recent changeful decade, these enclaves and those who inhabited them had continued to exist by exercising some power to resist change, or perhaps because no one found it worthwhile to remove them. They had been left on their own and forgotten, and it occurred to some that the mist of oblivion would hang over them forever.

USTAD RAMZI

Ustad Ramzi was the head of a pahalwan clan and the custodian of a wrestler's akhara. He was a man of frugal speech and austere habits, and appeared to some a stern man. His imposing stature, a heavyset jaw, and upturned whiskers only reinforced this impression. He was one of those men who do not accept the futility and emptiness of life, but who try continuously to give it meaning — a reflection of their own life's purpose.

Fifteen years earlier, in 1935, he had won the highest wrestling title in the land, Ustad-e-Zaman. This title was at the heart of a long struggle between Ustad Ramzi's clan and its rivals who had defended it for years. By winning the title, Ustad Ramzi had fulfilled the coveted dream of his clan elders. He had defended it many times since and cherished it as a sacred trust vouchsafed to the strength of his arms.

Recently, Ustad Ramzi's world had been shaken by the abolition of the princely states whose nawabs and rajas had traditionally patronized the wrestling arts. Many smaller akharas had closed down in consequence. The two surviving akharas belonging to Ustad Ramzi and his rival clan had also experienced the bite of hard times. Trainee pahalwans continued to take instruction, but there were fewer of them than before. Only a few bouts had been organized in the past year, and they had not drawn many spectators.

The prevailing situation made the future of this sport look uncertain, at best. These circumstances, however, had not affected Ustad Ramzi's unremitting adherence to his creed or checked his aspirations for the sport and its practitioners.

The akhara was a hallowed place for him, where a man made of clay came in contact with his essence. On the day he first put on the fighter's belt and stepped into the akhara, Ustad Ramzi made the pahalwan's traditional pledge to strive for the perfection of his body and soul until he returned to earth upon his death. The akhara, which his patriarchs had tended with their labour and sweat, was still the mainstay of his life. It had always been guided by the example of his elders, and as it was before, so it was now.

Ustad Ramzi had continued with his absolute ways in his diminishing sphere of influence where everything was predetermined, and every act, every gesture was of consequence. This consciousness had given a fatalistic decisiveness to his actions. People coping with the pressures of life after Partition, battling harsh circumstances with all the means in their possession – had neither the use nor sympathy for such intensity of purpose. Even those close to Ustad Ramzi sometimes found it difficult to understand or appreciate his motives. For many, Ustad Ramzi's set outlook on life had turned from a virtue to an impediment.

Adjacent to Ustad Ramzi's akhara was a private cemetery marked by an enclosure lined with cypresses, yews and banyans. It was a relic of the time when it was not unusual for people to be buried where they had worked and spent their lives. Besides Ustad Ramzi's ancestors, other pahalwans who had upheld the art's strict tenets were also honoured by being buried there.

Ustad Ramzi did not allow sweepers to enter the cemetery for fear of polluting the sanctity of its grounds; instead, he swept it himself every week with a broom of palm fronds. He never entered it without making ablutions. He kept the cemetery rimmed by rose boughs as a sign of devotion to the memory of his elders whose lives had been lived in strict conformity with their creed. He always experienced a deep sense of harmony in that place.

The graves were not laid symmetrically, and the ground was a little uneven and sloped to one side. In a corner at the acclivity of the slope, Ustad Ramzi had placed two stones and surmounted them with a marble slab to improvise a bench where he kept his gardening tools. Sitting there he could see the spot in the cemetery where lay his own unfilled grave. He had made it several years earlier and exulted in the anticipation that the day he was laid there, his life, too, would have conformed to that of his elders' existence and become a part of it.

In recent days, the enclosure that housed Ustad Ramzi's akhara and the adjacent cemetery was jestingly referred to as the Elephants' Graveyard – that mythical spot in a forest to which elephants retire at the approach of death. The caricature of the pahalwan as a dying beast and the implied suggestion that in the eyes and minds of people the pahalwan's art and his world were doomed, were not lost on Ustad Ramzi. The wedge of antipathy that had slowly been driven between him and the world had left Ustad Ramzi unruffled; he had learnt to take in disparaging words without feeling outrage.

TAMAMI

When the akhara was allotted to Ustad Ramzi's ancestors, its five buildings were used as living quarters by pahalwans and their retainers. Only three build-ings stood now, in varying stages of ruin. One had been locked up after its roof caved in. For some years swal-lows had nested there, along with the peacocks kept in the enclosure by Ustad Ramzi's father to exterminate the snakes that once infested the property. One building was used by the trainees. Ustad Ramzi and his younger brother Tamami lived in the other building which over-looked the akhara.

There was an age difference of twenty years between Ustad Ramzi and Tamami, and their temperaments and outlook on life were also greatly at variance. Tamami was of a frivolous nature. Unlike Ustad Ramzi, who took a nobler view of his art and creed, Tamami was more interested in the celebrity conferred by the title. While he was mostly neglectful of his duties as a pahalwan and had won neither honour nor renown for himself, he never let an opportunity pass to impress upon his friends and acquaintances that he was the scion of the clan in possession of the title. Tamami behaved as if he were himself the title holder.

The years of middle age had marked Ustad Ramzi's constitution. His hair was turning grey at the temples, the skin was beginning to wrinkle, and the joints of his bones were slowly being drained of their long resilience to pain. But Ustad Ramzi's devotion to his art remained unabated. Every morning before dawn he took the ewer from the niche in the wall and blessed the akhara clay by sprinkling it with blessed water. He then turned the clay in the pit, kneaded it with oil and herbs, and smoothed it before the trainees gathered to wrestle there. The modest tasks of turning and smoothing the akhara clay were as much a reminder for him of his pahalwan's pledge as they were an exercise in humility.

In recent years, at the approach of winter Ustad Ramzi felt the penetrating, dull throb of rheumatic pain which stiffened his knee joints and strained his walk. It sometimes kept him awake at night. His body had finally revolted against the prolonged use of arsenic, which he took to help digest a pahalwan's heavy diet. The year before, as winter progressed, the sharp pangs of pain he felt in his knees had gradually worsened, and made it difficult for him to finish his daily tasks in the akhara. In turning the clay, he still plied the mattock with a steady hand, and his back remained straight as a wood plank, but his knees could not hold up under stress in the same way. He did not tell anyone about his deteriorating health and carried on with his duties as before.

Ustad Ramzi's pride would not allow him to ask another to take on his duties. When he was a trainee pahalwan, even to have the privilege to ask for an important task one had to first prove oneself worthy of it. He was willing to be persuaded to delegate the tasks, but Tamami never asked to take them on. He merely expressed surprise at Ustad Ramzi's insistence on performing them himself when he could easily assign the work to one of the trainees.

Ustad Ramzi was disappointed by his brother's disregard of what his elders held a sacred ritual of their creed. He told himself that if Tamami failed to realize the importance and purpose of those humble rituals, he could never understand the essence of his creed. At the same time, Ustad Ramzi also saw the futility of pointing this out to Tamami. He knew that his brother had to come to that understanding on his own: only then could he understand the true significance of his existence, and find the conviction to make sacrifices for his art. Until such time he could not be trusted with the responsibilities of guarding the clan's interests to which Ustad Ramzi's own life was dedicated.

In the past, Ustad Ramzi had refused to discuss the delegation of tasks to others, but winter was upon him once again, and his knee pain had resurfaced. Almost overnight he had to learn the limits beyond which he could not exert his body.

Ustad Ramzi had delayed announcing his retirement in the hope that a day would come when the clan would find worthy hands to defend its honour after him – a day when he could hand over his place to Tamami and finally hang up his fighter's belt and retire. That day had not come.

Ustad Ramzi finally informed everyone in the clan that he would continue with his morning duty of blessing the akhara clay, and delegate to Tamami other duties such as the scheduling of trainees for preparing the akhara.

Tamami expressed happiness at his brother's decision and failed to notice the bitterness in Ustad Ramzi's smile.

Ustad Ramzi felt his vulnerability against the advance of disease and age keenly. He was still the title holder and the head of his clan, but from the day he made the announcement he knew that he would begin to lose his grip on the akhara affairs which he had run unchallenged for many years.

GOHAR JAN

Early in his professional career, Ustad Ramzi had realized that the entanglements of married life would not let him devote himself fully to his art and its exacting discipline. He vowed to remain celibate to achieve perfection in his art and shut his mind to thoughts of women. He finally attained the rank of an ustad or master, and acquired such celebrity that the mere privilege of being his sparring partner conferred eminence on a pahalwan. Throughout this time Ramzi observed his vow of celibacy.

The news of his visiting Gohar Jan's kotha in the courtesans' enclave was therefore received with great interest.

Gohar Jan was an accomplished singer whose raga recitals were renowned. Once a celebrated beauty, she was known for her haughty airs and capricious treatment of her lovers. Like other prominent tawaifs of her time, she maintained her own kotha where trainee girls or nayikas received instruction in the arts of musical entertainment. Gohar Jan's kotha in the inner city was the largest and most famed.

The young men frequented the kothas to learn the bearings of polite society, the older men to socialize, or rekindle the memories of their lost youth. Whenever one of them fell in love with a tawaif or a nayika, his affairs provided a spectacle and entertainment to the rest of them, until he was cured of his passion. Those who could not survive it did not return. A tawaif who fell in love had only two choices: she could either put an end to the association, or leave the kotha to pursue a life outside – if one was offered her. Implicit in the latter choice was the understanding that she would never be readmitted to the kotha if the promise of the new life failed her. There was a universe of failed unions, dreams, and abandoned hopes that started in the kothas and trailed off into the anonymity of the city's dark alleys. It was said – with some justification – that only the fickle survived in the kothas, and only the pitiless prospered.

When people heard the news of Ustad Ramzi's visits to Gohar Jan's kotha, they thought that like scores of others, he, too, was lured by Gohar Jan's physical charms. But there was another purpose to Ustad Ramzi's kotha visits.

Ustad Ramzi had been taken by an old acquaintance one evening to listen to Gohar Jan's mehfil of a raga recital at the kotha. That day, for the first time, he saw Gohar Jan as she entered with her nayikas and took her seat at the head of the ensemble of musicians. He saw her command her troupe quietly and imperiously, often with just a glance. That day, also for the first time, Ustad Ramzi felt the powerful meditative effect of music when Gohar Jan started a raga.

He had always struggled with a component of his discipline which stressed the need for meditation to focus physical strength. That chance visit to Gohar Jan's kotha made Ustad Ramzi understand how music could quieten the aggressive humours of his soul. He later returned to Gohar Jan's kotha and soon became one of the habitués of her mehfils.

Those who watched Ustad Ramzi for any signs of becoming infatuated with the tawaif were disappointed. At the end of the mehfil, he always left her kotha with others. Even after it was borne out that it was Ustad Ramzi's fondness for music which occasioned his visits to the kotha, that fact was not accepted. People made all kinds of insinuations: that Ustad Ramzi's endeavours outside the akhara did not meet with any success; that it is one thing to floor men, and another to contest the favours of a tawaif like Gohar Jan.

These comments inevitably reached Ustad Ramzi's ears, too, but he never learned that some people attributed these insinuations to Gohar Jan herself. Those who knew the tawaif could readily believe that it would have provided endless entertainment to Gohar Jan to make a spectacle of someone as self-absorbed and sacrosanct as Ustad Ramzi. But whether Gohar Jan found the sombre Ustad Ramzi too dull and uninteresting a quarry, or some other consideration hindered her, for some reason the insinuations ended there, and the gossip also died out.

For many years now Ustad Ramzi had regularly attended Gohar Jan's mehfils. He never realized that his visits to her kotha had now become for him a need; he felt restive without attending her mehfils once every few days. Over the years, the ragas themselves had been suffused with Gohar Jan's inflection and intonation; when Ustad Ramzi heard another's rendition, it hardly stirred a thing in his breast. It was as if the ragas only existed embodied in Gohar Jan's voice.

UNWORTHY HEIR

The akhara routines fell into disarray soon after Ustad Ramzi relinquished these duties to Tamami.

After a few weeks, the trainees slackened in their appointed chores. It was plain to see that they took their cue from Tamami. Instead of being the first to arrive at the akhara to supervise work, Tamami was often the last. And even then, he displayed no sense of urgency but idled away some more time talking to his friends from the neighbourhood. On some days the trainee who was supposed to turn the akhara clay would start late; on other days everyone would be held up because nobody had allotted the trainees their duties. The trainees had to wait for Tamami. In the meanwhile their bodies cooled down, and if they sparred without another warm-up they ended up with torn ligaments.

Even on the rare occasion when Ustad Ramzi saw Tamami get to the akhara early, he did not seem to exercise any control over the place. And yet, Tamami's exaggerated sense of self-worth seemed to have increased after Ustad Ramzi delegated many of the akhara's duties to him.

Ustad Ramzi witnessed his brother's fecklessness at every stage, and regarded Tamami's swagger and affectations as a contemptible substitute for character. The sight revolted him, and he bitterly regretted his decision to delegate the duties, notwithstanding the fact that he had been forced to do so by circumstances beyond his control.

Ustad Ramzi's inability to come to terms with this predicament, and the growing dread that he would now be at the mercy of others in matters which concerned him dearly, frequently made him despondent. The thought that the defence of the title of Ustad-e-Zaman and the future glory of his clan would fall on Tamami greatly disturbed Ustad Ramzi: in view of his brother's fickle nature and heedless ways, he doubted Tamami's ability to defend the title that was his clan's pride.

Reflecting on his many misfortunes Ustad Ramzi sometimes feared that, in the continuing decline of his art and clan, he may not have seen the last setback. As the custodian of his ancestors' akhara and clan's honour, he vowed to uphold his self-appointed destiny resolutely and at all costs.

KOTHA

Gohar Jan's stately and austere beauty had been mellowed somewhat by age. Her hazel green eyes were surrounded by wrinkles, and time had begun to cast her features in its soft, cruel mould. Her kotha still attracted patrons but the number of its visitors had dwindled.

That sudden and radical turnabout in life after Partition had created a deep feeling of uncertainty. A growing sense of frugality in all affairs had followed. It had adversely affected the fortunes of the tawaifs' enclave — a world that thrived on extravagance, and where people traditionally flaunted their wealth and fine taste.

The mehfils ended in many kothas. The drapes in the kothas remained drawn. The wooden staircases smelled of dampness. The carpets had not been aired in a long time and were musty. In the music rooms, tanpuras gathered dust under their silken wraps and their necks became bent from the humidity. The silence of the sarangis continued unbroken and the heads of the tablas and pakhavajs became wrinkled and dry. The quiet of the music rooms was broken sometimes by the sound of a string snapping.

The neighbourhood seemed more alive in daytime than at night. Most of the nayikas had moved out from the kothas to find a trade in which their training in the musical arts could advance a career. Many had joined the fledgling film industry. In the last year, two nayikas had left Gohar Jan's kotha. One had migrated. Another tried to open her own kotha in another neighbourhood, but failing to attract new patrons closed it down. Only one nayika, Malka, remained with Gohar Jan.

The only other occupant of the kotha was Gohar Jan's old retainer, Banday Ali, who had been associated with it for nearly three decades. He was in charge of the mehfils and also looked after the kotha's finances. Every evening he made sure that the paandans were stocked, the drinks ready, the white floor coverings spread in the Music Room, and bolsters placed for the guests. Two servants were also on hand to fill the hookahs for visitors, refresh them at regular intervals, and run errands if the guests wished to send for food from the bazaar or call a conveyance at the evening's end.

Banday Ali usually finished his preparations an hour before the mehfil started. Then he had his customary cup of tea before opening the doors of the kotha. After the musicians arrived he sat on his sofa at the entrance where he greeted visitors. Malka received the guests at the door of the Music Room, offered them paan, and ushered them in where the musicians were already seated and awaiting Gohar Jan.

At the end of the mehfil the guests left their payment in a money box. While the servants cleared up the room, Banday Ali did his accounting. After the house staff left he closed the kotha doors and retired to his room on the top floor of the building to sip his cup of opium.

Banday Ali regularly gave an account of the kotha's finances to Gohar Jan on the fifth of every month. But in recent days the exercise made him uncomfortable. Having been associated with the kotha and its finances for so long, he felt he was himself somehow to blame for its declining income.

Gohar Jan had been quietly selling her gold since the previous year to maintain the kotha on the same lavish scale as before. Banday Ali was the only person who knew about this. Gohar Jan had forbidden him from discussing it even with Malka. He had quietly suggested to

Gohar Jan a few times that she could rent out the kotha's western wing which had a separate entrance and was no longer occupied by the two nayikas. But each time Banday Ali made his suggestion Gohar Jan declined it with the same equanimity with which she received the account of her diminishing income.

MALKA

Gohar Jan's relationship with her nayika, Malka, was an unusual one, perhaps because of the special circumstances of her presence at the kotha. Unlike other nayikas who either joined kothas in their youth or were sold to the mistresses of the establishments, Malka had arrived at Gohar Jan's kotha as a foundling. One winter morning – twenty-three years earlier – Banday Ali had discovered the baby wrapped in a piece of felt cloth lying at the kotha entrance. Gohar Jan made every effort to find the mother, but had no success despite all her contacts and influence with the city administration. As Gohar Jan had feared, the orphanage refused to take in a child sent from the tawaifs' enclave.

Gohar Jan decided to raise the girl at the kotha. But she never showed her any fondness. Banday Ali, who saw no emotional bond between the two, mentioned to Gohar Jan a few times that the child needed more affection from those around her. He never received a response from Gohar Jan.

It was perhaps a result of Gohar Jan's frosty demeanour towards her that Malka herself grew up cold and reserved. She was pretty and her sharp features finely balanced her natural, graceful air but her manner was quiet and aloof. Even Banday Ali who nursed a filial feeling towards Malka saw that she did not return his affection with any warmth.

In view of Gohar Jan's impassive attitude towards Malka, Banday Ali could not understand why she gave her a room near her own living quarters instead of in the kotha's west wing reserved for the nayikas. The other nayikas saw that as an unfair privilege for Malka and it laid the foundations of constant animosity between them.

These were not the only contradictions Banday Ali saw in Gohar Jan's behaviour towards Malka. Gohar Jan did not impose the same strict discipline on her that she imposed on the other nayikas. In this instance, perhaps, it was also unnecessary. Malka submitted herself to the hard training in music and dance without persuasion.

Either from a sense of loneliness or competition with the other nayikas, she excelled at what she was taught. Gohar Jan offered encouragement to the other nayikas over their least achievements, but ignored Malka's hard work.

One day in the Music Room, Banday Ali witnessed yet another moment in the continuing drama as Malka underwent a training session with Gohar Jan.

'Straighten the left foot. Put the right hand...' Gohar Jan was explaining.

It was probably Gohar Jan's detached manner that made Malka restless. In the middle of her steps she did a pirouette.

Gohar Jan looked up.

'Why don't we begin with the pirouette?' Malka asked her.

'Does make-up start with the eyes or the feet? Do you put on the ankle-band before the head-adornment? That is why you start with the salutation and end with a pirouette. Like the sixteen adornments, the movements too follow a sequence...'

Even as she explained, Malka was moving her fingers in the imitation of a bird in flight.

Gohar Jan cast a reproving look at her and continued, 'All right. Put the right hand above your head in the shape of the half-moon. Stretch forward the left hand in a half circle... More composure!'

Malka kept looking straight at the wall in obstinate silence. There was a brief pause as Gohar Jan looked at her again.

'Very well,' Gohar Jan said. 'That is your lesson for today. Go and rest.'

Instead of leaving, Malka sat down and began strumming on the tanpura.

'What is this now?' Gohar Jan chided her. 'You won't rest, nor will you let me have any peace!'

Malka did not answer.

'Play it then if it is your wish,' Gohar Jan said half-heartedly.

Malka got up and left the room.

Banday Ali sometimes tried to compensate for Gohar Jan's disregard by praising Malka's talents to her. Malka would listen politely with her head lowered without expressing any joy. He could see that after being denied Gohar Jan's love as a child she now sought her praise as an adult. The more Gohar Jan ignored her, the harder Malka tried to win her attention. Banday Ali realized that no matter how much he might praise Malka it would never equal even a glance of appreciation from the one whose approval she sought.

Whenever Malka expressed a desire to perform before an audience, Gohar Jan summarily rejected the request, saying that Malka still had to learn a great deal.

For a brief period after the two nayikas left Gohar Jan's kotha, Banday Ali saw Malka happy. He felt, as did Malka, that she would finally have Gohar Jan's complete attention and be given an opportunity to perform. But even the departure of the other nayikas did not bring about any change in Gohar Jan's manner.

Banday Ali could not understand why Gohar Jan would not prepare Malka to take her place as the mistress of the kotha. Before the nayikas left Gohar Jan, she often told Banday Ali that she would soon appoint her successor. But since their leaving she had never brought up the subject again.

While Banday Ali could not always understand Gohar Jan's motives in her treatment of Malka, he knew that she never acted without careful thought. Banday Ali felt that even if Gohar Jan did not think that Malka had the talent or the acumen to become renowned in the musical arts, she should have at least allowed her an opportunity to prove herself. Why she denied Malka this chance remained a mystery to him. And while Malka regarded Gohar Jan with a mix of awe and reverence, Banday Ali felt that sooner or later her feelings towards Gohar Jan would turn sour.

COVETING AND ANXIETY

Ustad Ramzi's long reign as title holder had built an aura of infallibility around him, and Tamami had grown up in its shadow. Tamami remained in awe of his brother even when time began to take its own toll on Ustad Ramzi's legend and not many outside his neighbourhood remembered him as the champion who had defended his title consecutive times.

Grown accustomed to the taste of celebrity, Tamami coveted the title of Ustad-e-Zaman. He knew that upon Ustad Ramzi's retirement his title would be open to challenge. He felt confident about holding his own against the pahalwans of the rival clan. As Ustad Ramzi grew older Tamami expected him to step aside in order to allow him to take his place.

But he could see no signs of Ustad Ramzi hanging up his fighter's belt. Even after he had handed over some of the responsibilities at the akhara to him, he hadn't said a word about his plans to retire. Tamami asked himself why he should remain an underling, and feared that if Ustad Ramzi sensed that he had accepted his inferior standing, he might abandon his retirement plans altogether.

Tamami was beginning to tire of the wait and was losing interest in the akhara when one of Ustad Ramzi's old rivals, Imama, unexpectedly sent Ustad Ramzi a challenge.

Tamami felt Imama's challenge had given him an occasion to prove himself. As the title holder, Ustad Ramzi had the privilege to demand that his challenger fight one of his blood relations first. Tamami hoped that by nominating him, Ustad Ramzi would convey to everyone that the clan's honour was safe with Tamami, and he was equal to defending the title. It would be the turning point, Tamami thought, which might clear the way for his brother to step aside in his favour. Tamami was confident, too, of defeating Imama who was much older than he, and who, in Tamami's view, could not match his strength. Ustad Ramzi had defeated him three times in succession in defence of his title.

Ustad Ramzi was to declare his intent at a council of the elders of the clan. When it was held, Tamami learned that Ustad Ramzi had made the decision to accept Imama's challenge and fight him himself.

———

Imama's challenge had surprised Ustad Ramzi because it was not the usual practice for senior pahalwans to challenge someone who had defeated them three times.

Ustad Ramzi suspected a motive and remembered Imama's son who had been in training for some years. He had not seen him fight recently, but Ustad Ramzi had heard that he sparred with four trainees at a time. The elders of his clan considered him a natural fighter. If Imama were to defeat Ustad Ramzi, he could use the title holder's privilege to ask any challengers to first fight his son. Knowing that Ustad Ramzi would not fight a pahalwan who was low in the profession's hierarchy, Imama would make sure that the title remained with his clan.

The thought never crossed Ustad Ramzi's mind to nominate Tamami to fight Imama. Ustad Ramzi could not countenance appointing someone unworthy and imperfect to represent his clan. But people who only looked at the apparent age advantage Tamami would have had over Imama wondered why Ustad Ramzi had missed the opportunity to raise Tamami's profile and nominate him to fight Imama. As they knew Ustad Ramzi's actions to be beyond reproach and in his clan's best interests, they surmised that as a pahalwan Tamami must be too incapable and weak, and concluded that he would, then, have even less chance against Imama's son in the future. And so it began to be said that the bout's outcome would be a clear indication of how Ustad Ramzi's clan would fare in the future. This only increased Ustad Ramzi's apprehension about the vulnerability of his clan's honour.

Ustad Ramzi made his preparations to defend the title and hoped that his waning strength would not belie his skill. When he had last fought Imama five years ago the contraction of his muscles had been hidden under layers of fat and taut skin. There were wrinkles now on Ustad Ramzi's kneecaps, and his joints constantly gave him trouble. His stamina was also far inferior now. Imama was six years younger than him, and at their age, this made a considerable difference.

As the day of the bout approached and the severity of his exercises increased, the thought often crossed Ustad Ramzi's mind that he would have been spared the ordeal if Tamami had not been neglectful of his responsibilities. As he struggled to meet the hard standards he set for his training, Tamami's disregard for any duty towards his clan became ever more manifest to Ustad

Ramzi. When he saw Tamami near the akhara he felt he was only there from his concern about whether or not he would continue to bask in the glory of the clan's title. Tamami's presence began to annoy him and as the days progressed, his rancour towards his brother gradually increased.

———

The talk of Ustad Ramzi's distrust of his brother's ability reached Tamami — although nobody ever spoke directly to him. When asked about Ustad Ramzi's decision Tamami said that his brother was neither so weak nor so old as to need someone as a stand-in for his title defence. He thought this was all he could say without compromising his pride. He felt that Ustad Ramzi had wronged him, and his decision had made others think less of him — not only as a pahalwan but also as a brother.

Tamami sensed Ustad Ramzi's unhappiness about his presence in the akhara during his preparations. He found it hard to read his older brother's mind just as he had found it hard to come up to his expectations. But he knew that he would feel grievously insulted if Ustad Ramzi told him some day to keep away from the akhara during his preparations. Tamami kept out of Ustad Ramzi's way, although he did not wish others to think that at a time when his clan's title was at stake, he was not there to support his brother. He saw the injustice of his situation but could do nothing to change it, and his pride did not let him confide his feelings to any of his friends.

As the appointed day for the challenge bout approached, Tamami's feelings of self-pity were overcome by compassion for his brother, whom he saw exert himself daily despite his ebbing strength. Tamami forgot both his grievances and the fact that his brother had brought those rigours upon himself.

NEWCOMER

*Lately, **a new man**, **Hayat***, had been seen at Gohar Jan's kotha. His aspect and manners revealed someone absolutely unfamiliar with kotha etiquette. Gohar Jan sensed that he was ill at ease among the kotha's habitués who made no effort to welcome him into their small group. Hayat's inattentiveness to the recital did not escape her notice either. His gaze often travelled towards Malka who sat beside her and across from him.

Hayat did not linger at the end of the mehfil. He returned the following night and the next night as well.

After Hayat's third visit to the kotha, Malka approached Gohar Jan. Speaking softly and with lowered eyes, she said to her, 'The newcomer makes me uncomfortable.'

Gohar Jan did not answer. She had made her inquiries about the man and his background. Hayat was a real-estate developer who had come to the inner city to survey and bid on the newly introduced residential development schemes. He was not known in the tawaifs' enclave. She assumed curiosity had brought him there.

Another week passed. Hayat still paid little attention to Gohar Jan's recital, but he did not stare at Malka impertinently as he had done on the first few occasions. When he came upstairs he sometimes attempted to make conversation with Malka on the way to the Music Room. During the mehfils he seemed preoccupied and thoughtful.

Gohar Jan continued to countenance Hayat's behaviour, but she saw that the other visitors who noticed Hayat's interest in Malka and Gohar Jan's indulgence of it were gossiping about it. The men could not solicit Malka's favours as she had not started performing yet. They saw in Gohar Jan's tolerance of Hayat's breach of kotha etiquette an unjust show of favour to the newcomer.

After visiting the kotha continuously for three weeks Hayat stopped coming. Malka was unable to disguise her growing unease and disquiet. Her nervous movements betrayed her inner anxiety. Things dropped from her hands. When entering or leaving rooms she would bump into doors and walls like someone unsure of her bearings. She was in a heightened state of anxiety for more than a week, and when Hayat did not return Malka sank into a state of gloom. Her verve and energy were sapped; she became introverted and quiet.

Gohar Jan, who had smiled to herself at Malka's restlessness earlier, now regarded her with concern. But even as she worried about Malka, she did not show it.

In the fifth week after the stranger's first appearance at the evening mehfil someone knocked at the kotha door and Banday Ali opened the door to find Hayat standing on the landing.

When he entered and announced Hayat's presence, Malka was sitting with Gohar Jan. She rose to her feet in a sudden rush of agitation and excitement, her face flushed with happiness. Gohar Jan sent Malka to the adjoining room and asked Banday Ali to send in Hayat. She had been expecting him for the last few weeks. She had found out that he had not left the city.

She noticed the pallid look on Hayat's face as he entered. He seemed weak and exhausted. Casting a glance at Banday Ali, Hayat asked Gohar Jan if he might have a word in private. Banday Ali left them alone in the Music Room.

Hayat remained closeted with Gohar Jan for nearly an hour. At the end of their meeting, Gohar Jan went into the adjoining chamber and led Malka by the hand into the Music Room. Hayat rose as Malka entered. After the two had sat down, Gohar Jan left them together, and went out onto the terrace where she found Banday Ali. She sat down on the sofa and told him of the decision she had made about Malka's future.

Banday Ali collapsed on the wooden bench near the flowerpots on the terrace. He stared at Gohar Jan but her categorical silence did not allow him to speak. His opium addiction had dulled Banday Ali's responses and quieted his emotions. He looked confused and shocked.

A half-hour later, Hayat came out of the Music Room and had a brief exchange with Gohar Jan. After he left she returned to the Music Room, stopping for a moment to compose herself in the large mirror that hung in the corridor. Banday Ali remained on the terrace.

Gohar Jan found Malka where she had left her. Her body convulsed gently from her muffled sobs. Tears flowed through her fingers with which she covered her face. Gohar Jan sat down beside her.

'Why do you want me to leave?' Malka asked, looking uncomprehendingly at Gohar Jan.

'It was not I who suggested it. But it is for the best. You will be happy with him,' Gohar Jan said. After a brief hesitation she took Malka's hands into hers and pressed them gently.

Surprised, Malka looked up.

'How do you know that?' Malka asked. She left her hands in Gohar Jan's.

'You know it yourself. Don't tell me you don't.' Gohar Jan spoke with her usual self-control, looking into Malka's eyes.

She then averted her gaze and left Malka's side.

A change had come over Gohar Jan. Banday Ali saw it as she came out of the Music Room and worried for her.

———

A week after Malka left the tawaifs' enclave as Hayat's bride, an increasingly confused and agitated Banday Ali tried to reconcile himself with the bitter prospect of never seeing her again. While handing Gohar Jan his monthly report on the kotha's finances, he confronted her.

'If it was Malka's happiness you sought, surely you could see how happy it would have made her if you allowed her to perform. You never did.'

Gohar Jan silently looked through the accounts.

'Not once, Gohar Jan,' Banday Ali said. 'You did not allow her to perform even once. You denied her all she had longed for since she was a child.'

Gohar Jan now looked up and met Banday Ali's angry gaze.

'How could I, Banday Ali?' Gohar Jan said slowly. 'How could I impose a destiny on her, or tie her to the kotha with any bonds? Don't you realize she was given to me in trust.'

With those words Gohar Jan finally answered every question Banday Ali had asked himself for the last twenty-three years on the subject of the girl who had been abandoned at the kotha's steps, and Gohar Jan's treatment of her.

Gohar Jan's statement left Banday Ali deeply perplexed. It would have baffled anyone who knew her as well as Banday Ali did, and thought her dedication to the kotha life and her art to be absolute and above all other considerations.

Banday Ali did not say anything. He needed time to mull over in silence what Gohar Jan had said. But as he turned to go something occurred to him. He stopped, looked at Gohar Jan, and asked, 'What if the promise of happiness turns out to be false for her? What if she returns, Gohar Jan?'

Gohar Jan spoke softly and reluctantly, as if uttering the words might make the dreaded thing happen. 'If she returned, Banday Ali... she could have what is not allowed any tawaif in the same circumstances: she could have the life she thought she wanted.'

CHALLENGE

About a month before Ustad Ramzi's scheduled bout,
Tamami took along some trainees and visited Imama's
neighbourhood. There they ran into a group of pahalwans from Imama's clan. The exchange of taunts between the two rival groups became heated.

The noise reached Imama's nearby akhara, and Imama
came out with his son and clan members to investigate.
He tried to break up the quarrel but Tamami used the
opportunity to challenge him to a bout. The trainees
in Tamami's group started shouting with joy. Imama's
son pushed forward to accept the challenge instead, but
Tamami refused, claiming his right to fight Imama as
the blood brother of the title holder.

This unexpected challenge surprised Imama and his clan. They smelled a conspiracy in Tamami's visit. They had heard rumours that Ustad Ramzi was using turmeric poultices on his knees to alleviate pain, and was not doing some of the leg-exercises usually included in the preparations for a bout. They suspected Ustad Ramzi was afraid of facing Imama and had tried to evade the showdown by setting up Imama against Tamami.

Tamami had challenged Imama before his clan. Imama could have used his authority as a senior pahalwan to spurn the challenge, but by refusing the challenge of Ustad Ramzi's blood brother he risked losing face.

Imama nodded to his trainers. They told Tamami that the next morning their clan elders would call on Ustad Ramzi to settle the details of the bout.

In a jubilant mood, Tamami started for his akhara with his retinue of trainees. One of the pahalwans in their group borrowed a bicycle from a friend and pedalled away to take the news to Ustad Ramzi.

When Tamami and his friends, and a few other trainees who had joined them on their way, drew close to the akhara, they found Ustad Ramzi waiting for them at the gate.

'Who gave you permission to go to Imama's akhara and challenge him? Who gave you leave?'

Everyone became silent.

'Ustad...' Tamami looked stupefied by Ustad Ramzi's outburst. 'I was just passing by when...'

'Don't lie to me!' Ustad Ramzi roared.

Tamami's jubilant spirits died. Sensing that he had committed something unforgivable, he decided to confess.

'I went there to challenge him, Ustad,' Tamami said softly.

'You do not have the freedom to challenge Imama. You are no match for him. You will bring disgrace to the clan if you fight him.' Ustad Ramzi's words rang in the akhara.

'I did it for the clan,' Tamami retorted, mustering his failing courage. 'I can defeat Imama!'

'It was not your place. I am the head of the clan. Never again interfere in matters that are my responsibility. I am not dead yet.'

Tamami made an effort to sound confident. 'I can defeat Imama!'

One of the trainees shouted, 'Tamami *will* defeat Imama, Ustad Ramzi, you'll see.'

'Go back to your rooms, you idiots! You have to wake up early tomorrow morning,' Ustad Ramzi shouted at the trainees.

Leaving them standing there, Ustad Ramzi returned to his room and the trainees retired to their quarters with Tamami. When they had recovered from the outburst they tried to cheer Tamami up, but Ustad Ramzi's rebuke had crushed him. He slept in the trainees' quarters that night.

The next day Imama's clan elders called on Ustad Ramzi to settle the details. The bout was to be held within ten days at an industrial plot rented for the purpose. A man named Gulab Deen who had recently set himself up as a sports promoter agreed to publicize the event.

———

Tamami's enthusiasm for the fight with Imama had begun to wane from the moment Ustad Ramzi rebuked him. He made his preparations for the encounter but his heart was no longer in it, even though he wished to prove his brother wrong.

Ustad Ramzi had changed the time for his exercises and removed his exercise equipment from the centre of the akhara so that Tamami could have the place in the morning hours. But he did not supervise Tamami's exercises as some had expected. When approached by his clan elders, Ustad Ramzi refused. He made no secret of his reasons for doing so either: 'To train him myself for this fight,' he said, 'would be the same as to approve his actions. I will not be able to show Imama my face if I did.'

The clan elders no longer pressed Ustad Ramzi. Kabira, a senior pahalwan, was appointed as Tamami's trainer instead.

DISDAIN

On the day of the bout, Ustad Ramzi did not accompany Tamami to the akhara. When Kabira came to request his attendance, Ustad Ramzi only replied: 'I will not go to witness my clan's humiliation!'

After consulting with the elders of both clans, promoter Gulab Deen had made admissions free. Although few people turned up to see the fight, the stout promoter looked happy. Promoters were a new phenomenon in the sport. When the introductions were made, Gulab Deen used the occasion to talk about his work.

Imama stood calmly with his trainer, but his son glared at Tamami with ill-concealed hostility.

The fight itself barely lasted a few minutes. As Tamami was making an attempt to secure a hold, Imama threw him off balance. Following with a powerful sweep of his legs Imama toppled him over. As he fell, both of Tamami's shoulders touched the ground. Only when Tamami saw Kabira entering the akhara did he understand that it was over. It all happened so quickly that he did not even have time to realize that he had lost.

Imama's jubilant clan surrounded him. His son stepped towards Tamami, but Imama stopped him, and pulled him away. Tamami was galled by the triumphant and disdainful look in his eyes.

Imama was carried in a procession to his akhara, on the shoulders of his clan members.

Feeling too ashamed to return to the akhara, Tamami spent the night at Kabira's house. Later in the afternoon of the next day, when he knew Ustad Ramzi would be taking his rest, Tamami returned to the enclosure.

A few trainees were exercising in the akhara. Ustad Ramzi came out of his room but ignored him. Tamami noticed that Ustad Ramzi's exercise equipment had been returned to the centre of the akhara.

———

When Imama and his clan did not see Ustad Ramzi at the bout, they realized that Tamami's challenge to Imama was not orchestrated by him. Nevertheless, rumours about a conspiracy hatched by Ustad Ramzi continued to spread.

'Ustad Ramzi may have defeated Imama in the past but now he is too old to wrestle with him. He used Tamami to stop him but failed.'

'Ustad Ramzi planned it so that Tamami could avoid fighting Imama's son. Now, neither Ustad Ramzi nor Tamami have a chance against them.'

'Ustad Ramzi had carefully thought it out. He wanted Tamami to earn some prestige by taking on a safe bet. He miscalculated badly in thinking that old Imama would cede easily to an inexperienced pahalwan like Tamami.'

If there was anything that bothered Ustad Ramzi more than the rumours, it was the thought that he had to listen to these imprecations on account of Tamami. Ustad Ramzi was glad that finally he did not have to see Tamami's face during his own preparations. Tamami kept away from the akhara while he exercised.

Only a few days remained before his bout with Imama.

CLOSURE

Nearly half the furniture of Gohar Jan's kotha had been sold. The rooms from which it had been removed were locked up so that the visitors did not witness the bare walls and floors. But the void and bareness spilled out of the rooms and compounded the emptiness Banday Ali felt from Malka's absence.

It was only after Malka had left that Banday Ali truly understood how hard it had been for Gohar Jan to constantly wear a mask of indifference and curb the least expression of affection and warmth towards Malka to make sure she did not become emotionally attached to her or the kotha in any way. Atonement was never possible for Gohar Jan. But after Malka's departure, the guilt of denying her the love she sought exacted a great emotional cost on her; within a fortnight she seemed to have aged many years.

She asked Banday Ali to remove everything that might remind her of Malka. All of Malka's furniture was locked away in the girl's room.

Then Gohar Jan took ill and the mehfils at the kotha were cancelled for the first time. Gohar Jan's physical illness was perhaps her body's way to staunch her inner suffering. She slowly recuperated and resumed her mehfils. Banday Ali noticed, though, that there were days when she became very quiet and spent hours lying in bed, deep in reflection.

When she informed Banday Ali of her decision to discontinue the mehfils, Banday Ali could only nod silently. Especially in her condition, the long recitals were too exhausting.

Ustad Ramzi was kept away by his preparations for the bout on the day Gohar Jan made the announcement to end the mehfils at her kotha, and he was still away when the last mehfil was held. Banday Ali did not have an opportunity to inform Ustad Ramzi of the change. For a moment he considered sending him a message, but he thought that sooner or later the report would reach him.

ENCOUNTER

Tamami's defeat by Imama and rumours about the imminent downfall of Ustad Ramzi's clan seemed to have revived people's interest in the bout. In contrast to Tamami's fight with Imama, a bigger crowd had gathered at the exhibition grounds a day before Ustad Ramzi and Imama's fight to see the trainees from both clans prepare the akhara.

They had cleared the debris from the field and sprinkled the grounds with water to settle the dust. The akhara clay had been turned several times to remove lumps, and later kneaded with turmeric and aromatic herbs. The area was roped off and covered with jute sacks. In the evening the rings for spectators were marked around the akhara with powdered limestone.

The elders of the two clans had decided to keep the entry open for the bout to encourage maximum attendance. Gulab Deen, who visited the site, walked around with a martyr's look since his services were not engaged for the event.

On the morning of the bout pitchers of sardai, prepared with almonds, milk and herbs, and platters of dried dates were taken to the grounds to be served to the spectators.

In the enclosure Ustad Ramzi put on his fighting drawers. A white turban fumigated with incense was tied on his head by an elder of the clan and his shoulders were draped with a coverlet embroidered with Quranic verses. Tamami and the trainees carried him to the exhibition ground on their shoulders, reciting the *qasida burda* to solicit an auspicious outcome.

Ustad Ramzi felt a vague foreboding as the procession approached the akhara, but he was pleased to see the large crowd that had gathered to witness the bout.

People filled the expanse of the exhibition grounds and some had climbed on to the boundary walls and the trees to have a better view. A festive mood prevailed among the trainees of the two clans. The two champions entered the exhibition grounds at the same time amid the uproar of their supporters and the crowd. The noisy crowd gradually became silent as the competitors were called for introductions.

When the bout began, Imama opened with defensive play. Ustad Ramzi's clan cheered at this apparent hint of weakness, but Ustad Ramzi immediately saw Imama's intention of protracting the fight. A longer bout would be to Imama's advantage as his younger body would get progressively warmer, more limber, and feel less pain. Ustad Ramzi knew his own stamina would decline in the same proportion, and if he tried to hasten the pace he would spend his energies sooner and make mistakes. He relaxed his mind and prepared himself for a prolonged fight knowing well that his days of epic contests, when he could grapple with opponents for hours, were behind him.

Both pahalwans were tired by the end of the first half-hour. Imama had applied two takedowns successfully, though he came very close to being pinned down once by his rival. Ustad Ramzi had decided not to resist Imama's strategy for the first several moves, hoping Imama might make mistakes if he realized that Ustad Ramzi had seen through his plan and was not unnerved. But instead of changing his strategy Imama fortified it with prolonged, defensive moves.

Imama was drenched in perspiration, but his breathing was unaffected. Ustad Ramzi's breath came unevenly now and he knew that it couldn't have escaped Imama's notice.

Their next few movements succeeded each other in a flash. Imama lunged forward to apply a takedown. Ustad Ramzi countered it and gripped his rival's neck. Imama answered with a defensive lock.

After a few moments of remaining thus engaged, Ustad Ramzi felt a severe throbbing in his temples. It became progressively painful. He knew he would not be able to maintain his lock much longer.

Meanwhile, seeing that Imama was unable to break Ustad Ramzi's hold, the referee conferred with the judges and came over to ask Imama if he wished to disengage. If either of the pahalwans had chosen to disengage, the fight would have been declared a tie. Imama waved his arm angrily in refusal. Respecting his adversary's wishes, Ustad Ramzi also refused.

Some more time passed. The throbbing in Ustad Ramzi's temple had now become unbearable. The impatient shouts of the spectators worsened the pain and each pulse felt like a hammer stroke in his skull. Only now he felt conscious of a spasm in his left knee, as if someone had stuck a jagged knife into it. That was the least of his worries because he felt Imama's body cooling down under him. Imama had not made another move, knowing he was exhausting Ustad Ramzi's strength just by lying there. Ustad Ramzi realized Imama was marshalling his energies to apply another reversal; he had refused to disengage for good reason.

A few moments later Ustad Ramzi saw one of the elders of Imama's clan regarding Imama intently. Ustad Ramzi noticed an exchange between him and Imama's son. Ustad Ramzi was distracted when he noticed that Tamami had moved closer to the akhara. His brother's anxious gaze settled on Ustad Ramzi who averted his eyes.

Ustad Ramzi again noticed an exchange between Imama and his clan elder who had come closer to see how Imama was holding up. Imama gesticulated furiously a few moments later.

There seemed to be some confusion as the elder walked up to the judges and Imama's son tried to hold him back. Ustad Ramzi felt a sudden movement under him and realized Imama was exerting himself to break loose. Ustad Ramzi felt a cramp developing in his arm. He knew that, once free, Imama could easily press his back to the clay since his energies were already spent. Ustad Ramzi marshalled all his remaining strength and tightened his hold, knowing well that his strength was failing him.

At that moment Ustad Ramzi clearly saw the end of his reign and the loss of his title. He felt too mentally exhausted to think further and resigned himself to his circumstances.

Imama broke free the moment the drumming of the dhol signalled the end of the bout. It had been declared a tie. The two were to fight again within three months. In the meanwhile, the title remained with Ustad Ramzi.

The flow of blood in Ustad Ramzi's arm was obstructed from the tightness of his hold. It had gone numb. As Ustad Ramzi stood silently in a corner of the akhara rubbing his arm, he finally understood what might have been happening towards the end of the bout. Imama could not have seen the first gesture of his clan elder as perspiration streamed into his eyes. He only noticed the gesture when asked if he wished to continue a second time. Imama was unable to articulate the words properly as the pressure of Ustad Ramzi's hold had constricted his neck. The elder had misjudged the situation, thinking that the pressure was causing Imama's vision to black out. He asked the judges to stop the fight, thinking that Imama would ultimately benefit, as it would be declared a tie. He disregarded the request by Imama's son to wait a little longer.

Although Imama never spoke a word then or afterwards about what had happened, Ustad Ramzi understood why Imama had been furious. A simple misunderstanding had snatched victory from him.

Ustad Ramzi's gaze now travelled down his leg. He noticed the torn skin around his left kneecap. Smeared in clay, clots of blood and fat hung from the wound. He disregarded it. His thoughts returned to the last moments of the bout when he had seen defeat and accepted it. It was the weakest moment of his life.

Just then he felt someone's hand on his shoulder, and turned to find Tamami standing by his side. Tamami had tears in his eyes as he quietly embraced Ustad Ramzi. His presence there annoyed Ustad Ramzi.

'Get rid of your tears!' he snapped, breaking away from him.

Tamami withdrew without a word.

RIVAL

Imama and his clan seemed to have been marked for adversity. A week after drawing the fight with Ustad Ramzi, his son lost one of his legs in a road accident that ended his career. Imama held himself together as best he could, but was seen less and less often at the akhara until he stopped coming altogether.

Friends and foes alike said Ustad Ramzi could now rest assured his title was secure. Ustad Ramzi made no comment, but he did not believe it was the end of the matter. He put himself in Imama's place and wondered if he would rest for long, even taking into account the personal tragedy, upon discovering that his adversary was weak.

He realized that for the first time his clan had come close to losing its title. He was the first and only line of defence; at his age he was no longer infallible. Were it not for Tamami's weakness, he could have chosen the strategy Imama planned to use against him, and move Tamami into the first line of defence.

———

Not long afterwards Ustad Ramzi yielded to Tamami the charge of instructing the trainees as well. Tamami readily took it on but he did not have the necessary patience and perseverance needed in a trainer. After explaining a procedure once or twice he left the trainees by themselves. He lost his temper if he saw them repeat their mistakes.

When Ustad Ramzi heard the news that one of the trainees had stopped coming after an altercation with Tamami, he ordered Tamami go to the trainee's house and bring him back. Tamami acquiesced with bad grace.

———

Autumn gave way to winter and a faint mist began draping the neighbourhood in the mornings. Ustad Ramzi slept lightly. He was up a few hours before dawn broke. From the akhara he retired to the cemetery where he tended the roses before going to his quarters to rest. He came out after Tamami had finished his first set of exercises. Ustad Ramzi would sit on the seat by the akhara to get the daily report from Kabira. By that time Tamami would begin his second set of exercises.

Tamami often witnessed Ustad Ramzi giving instructions or demonstrating manoeuvres as he exercised. Once Tamami had been grappling with two trainees for half an hour. He was covered with clay, which coursed down his body along with streams of sweat. As he wheeled around and shook off one of the trainees from his back, he lost his balance and his hips touched the floor. Tamami recovered quickly, but at that moment Ustad Ramzi entered the akhara to demonstrate the move.

Tamami had felt himself in control when sparring with the trainees. That feeling disappeared when Ustad Ramzi stepped into the akhara. Tamami relinquished his hold on the trainee and they rose.

Ustad Ramzi balanced himself on his arms and knees and the trainees took their places to recreate the hold, which Tamami could not resolve perfectly. Ustad Ramzi identified the correct technique and, without losing his balance, threw down both trainees using the same manoeuvres Tamami had applied. Tamami watched Ustad Ramzi's manoeuvre carefully and nodded. The trainees praised Ustad Ramzi's skill. Tamami's friends and a few of the other pahalwans also made comments.

'How simple Ustad Ramzi made it look.'

'It is not without reason that he is the Ustad-e-Zaman.'

'Just wait until Tamami becomes Ustad-e-Zaman,' one of Tamami's friends casually remarked.

Everyone in the akhara became silent when the words were uttered. Tamami's friend realized his indiscretion and became quiet.

Ustad Ramzi looked at Tamami, who was trying to catch his breath after the long sparring session and had only vaguely heard what was said. He looked back blankly when he met Ustad Ramzi's searching glance.

A smile appeared on Ustad Ramzi's lips. He patted his brother's shoulder and vigorously embraced him.

'Ustad Ramzi and Tamami are going to grapple.' A voice spoke from the crowd.

'The brothers are going to have a match!' someone else said.

Tamami realized they had mistaken Ustad Ramzi's embrace for a grappling lock. Ustad Ramzi also regarded the trainees with a surprised look.

'Come see Ustad Ramzi and Tamami fight!' The excited babble continued.

Ustad Ramzi looked at Tamami and said, 'Be prepared.'

Tamami nodded a little awkwardly. He felt too great an anxiety at that moment to think with clarity. The brothers had not fought recently. Tamami feared Ustad Ramzi would overpower him and everyone would be a witness to his weakness. He felt his energy draining away.

Ustad Ramzi slapped his shoulder with his hands and took up a fighting stance. Tamami's hands also flew to Ustad Ramzi's shoulders.

The two of them leaned forward, their temples pressed together. The backs of their heads were level with each other and their eyes riveted to the floor. The trainees closed in around the akhara to watch.

As Tamami pushed with his body to secure the hold for an overhead drag he felt Ustad Ramzi resist. Then Tamami felt he was losing balance as his powerful thrust suddenly broke Ustad Ramzi's stance. Tamami recovered quickly.

The crowd silently witnessed the struggle without fully comprehending the situation. In that silence Tamami heard his heartbeat and Ustad Ramzi's breathing which maintained a broken rhythm.

His continuous deference to his brother's authority and belief in his infallible strength had instilled a sense of inferiority and inadequacy in Tamami. As the myth of Ustad Ramzi's strength was now shattered, the shadow under which Tamami had walked was also lifted. He realized he was his brother's superior in strength. He savoured the sense of power.

Ustad Ramzi did not wait for Tamami's move. He applied the overhead drag Tamami had intended. Before Ustad Ramzi could finish, however, Tamami countered by uncoiling his body and aggressively grasping Ustad Ramzi's arm in a lock.

Ustad Ramzi laughed nervously as he struggled to rise.

Tamami quickly let go.

'Yes! Yes! When did the young lion ever turn away before the old?' Ustad Ramzi said. 'But the old lion is not done yet. Come!'

Tamami could not overcome his feelings. Even as Ustad Ramzi spoke, their arms again locked together, Tamami rolled Ustad Ramzi's arm to break its grip on his elbow, then applied the drag, simultaneously stepping in to throw him down. Ustad Ramzi managed to use the counter-drag in time, and both of them hit the clay with Ustad Ramzi on top.

'I shall take some rest,' Ustad Ramzi spoke in a strained voice as he got up and patted Tamami's back. Before stepping out of the akhara he turned towards the trainees and said, 'You should continue exercising until Tamami gives you leave.'

Tamami contended with his conflicting emotions.

He was glad that Ustad Ramzi's redrag had foiled his move and saved him the shame. He had proved himself stronger than his brother but in the midst of applying the manoeuvre, he realized that he was about to floor his elder brother and the champion of the clan. It would have been an unforgivable act of disrespect.

And yet, Tamami felt an inner satisfaction. Now he has proof of my strength, he told himself. Those who have witnessed it also know now who is stronger. They won't be able to say that the clan's title would be in unworthy hands.

As Ustad Ramzi walked away Tamami saw how consumed and decayed he looked. The signs of ageing were visible on his body. His brother's physical weakness filled Tamami's heart with revulsion.

STRATEGY

After his encounter with Tamami that day, Ustad Ramzi went straight to the cemetery.

The incident in the akhara kept replaying itself in his mind's eye. He hadn't grappled with Tamami for a few months and it was a shock to realize that his brother was now physically stronger. As they stood locked in the tie-up position, Ustad Ramzi had felt the iron grip of Tamami's hands around his neck. Tamami's powerful thrust and the immense surge of strength flowing from his body had broken his stance. He had strained to answer Tamami's push and failed.

In the brief moment when Tamami paused, two thoughts raced through Ustad Ramzi's mind: that

Tamami's strength must be carefully adorned with skill to make him the protector of his clan's honour, and that he could now put his mind at rest about his clan's future. Later, as Tamami applied the aggressive countermove, the joy that had filled Ustad Ramzi's heart left it without a trace.

Tamami's intention to floor him had been too obvious.

Ustad Ramzi asked himself why it had happened. He saw his strength and Tamami's as an entity, meant to strive in unison, not as counterweights. He had never considered that he was pitting his strength against his brother as a rival. After delegating his akhara duties to Tamami and trusting his brother with instructing the trainees, he had kept him under his own instruction to improve his skill. Tamami had not appreciated that. It troubled Ustad Ramzi.

It was not an incident that he could attribute to Tamami's immaturity. Ustad Ramzi was sure it flowed from some base instinct.

It convinced him that Tamami judged himself and others by the criterion of strength alone. Tamami, whom he wished to become worthy of representing his clan's tradition, had again proven incapable of aspiring to the higher rewards of the art. That was the reason for his ignominious defeat at Imama's hands and for the incident in the akhara that day. Ustad Ramzi knew that for such men power remained the only ideal. The more they felt it stir inside their bodies, the more confident they felt of themselves.

Ustad Ramzi realized he could not relinquish his place to someone who neither showed deference to his tradition and elders nor understood the subtle points of skill. But he could turn Tamami's failings to the clan's advantage by changing the focus of his training to the cultivation of strength alone. Tamami would not become a consummate pahalwan once set on that course, but he would have the disproportionate strength necessary to block any challengers to the clan's title. Ustad Ramzi would never let it be said that the title was lost to his clan while he lived.

Ustad Ramzi's mind was finally decided. He thought no more about the akhara incident and spent the afternoon tending the rose bushes.

SOLITUDE

The acrid smell of the wilted jasmine flowers in the copper bowl, and the sight of the perfume-soaked cotton plugs in the glass bowl reminded Gohar Jan of Malka who used to arrange them for the mehfils. Something told her she would not return.

Gohar Jan had foreseen Malka going away from her life and was reconciled to it when it occurred. With her decision never to attach herself to any one man, Gohar Jan had also prepared herself for a life of solitude. She had assumed that it was not given to her to find satisfaction in a relationship. She found it instead in a discipline that needed a similar degree of tending and self-sacrifice. Now, that satisfaction was being replaced with anxiety.

Gohar Jan had been unprepared for the possibility of the kotha closing down because it had come about through a series of unforeseeable events. She felt helpless in quelling the feeling of loss that grew inside her. The passions and the energy of the kotha life and its glamour had given her life a sense of purpose and contentment, and its charms had sustained her in her womanhood's prime and beyond; it had become her only reference to life.

Now that the unforeseen had come about, Gohar Jan's impending solitude made her feel vulnerable and uncertain. She thought about the furrowed faces of old tawaifs sitting idly in their dark kothas waiting for their lives to end. She realized that she was now one of them.

Like waking from a dream broken in disquiet, she was unable to ward off her feeling of despair at the snapping of the thread that connected her past, present and future. She felt restive and disoriented. Sometimes the walls, the furniture, even the Music Room where she had performed for decades, appeared unfamiliar. It seemed that the kotha had a secret life of its own that was extinguished when she closed its doors.

She wondered if she might have felt a greater sense of her life's completeness if there had been someone to share it with her. She had never tried to answer this question before. Even the act of posing it might have been a tacit admission that she felt her life had been lacking. But with the boundaries of her world shrunk to the walls of her abode, and left with only a memory of the hustle and bustle of the kotha in days past, Gohar Jan was faced with the futility of her life's endeavour and her life's meaning. She could no longer escape it.

Shortly after the closure of Gohar Jan's kotha, two remaining kothas also closed down. Evenings in the tawaifs' enclave were finally silenced.

Their world no longer existed; but the tawaifs carried it within them in their memories, like exiles, and continued to adhere to a ritual of their lives. As before, they devoted the first act of the day to the vocal meditations of riyazat. The sound of their voices and their change of tone, timbre and pitch still resonated in the tawaifs' enclave at dawn. Gohar Jan, too, would get up at an early hour and sit down for her vocal meditations, but they brought her no satisfaction, no sense of peace.

VISIT

The servant girl surprised Gohar Jan by announcing the arrival of Ustad Ramzi one evening. Gohar Jan could not understand the reason for his visit.

The servant girl had answered the door as Banday Ali was away on an errand. Without knowing or asking the reason for Ustad Ramzi's visit, she had conducted him into the Music Room where Gohar Jan received guests. She found Ustad Ramzi standing in confusion at the entrance of the Music Room.

'I believe I'm early today...' Ustad Ramzi addressed Gohar Jan as soon as he saw her. 'Unless, there's some change,' he added uneasily.

Gohar Jan realized that Ustad Ramzi was unaware

of the news of the kotha's closure. 'I regret the inconvenience,' she said hesitantly. 'The mehfils ended some weeks ago. I am sorry you were not informed.'

Ustad Ramzi stared at her.

Something reminded Gohar Jan of a time many years ago when Ustad Ramzi had first started visiting her kotha. He rarely spoke, though he might commit to a word or two if someone sought his opinion. After her recital ended he would stay only as long as propriety demanded, and leave after putting his contribution in the moneybox. It was on one of those days that, amused by his demeanour, and acting on a sudden impulse, Gohar Jan had attempted to break through his reserve. He did not react. She desisted when she found out that Ustad Ramzi's strict formality was guided by his dedication to his art and vows of celibacy. From that day she received him in the same courteous manner as her other patrons, but never sought to further cultivate his acquaintance.

The servant re-entered to ask Gohar Jan if she needed anything.

'I must leave...' Ustad Ramzi said before he was interrupted by Gohar Jan.

'Please uncover the sitar,' she said to the servant girl.

She saw Ustad Ramzi looking enquiringly as the girl removed the protective brocade cover from Gohar Jan's sitar.

'Please sit down, Ustad Ramzi,' Gohar Jan said.

'Bring some water for Ustad Ramzi,' Gohar Jan addressed the servant girl. 'That would be all.'

Ustad Ramzi sat down reluctantly.

Gohar Jan would have found it indecorous to send Ustad Ramzi away without some token of hospitality after he was shown in by mistake, but it was on an impulse that she had asked him to stay.

When the servant girl brought water, Ustad Ramzi emptied it in one gulp.

Gohar Jan held up the sitar.

She noticed Ustad Ramzi was unable to concentrate during her recital. The news about the end of the mehfils had disturbed him deeply. As someone who had learned how painful it was to end a lifelong routine that gave purpose to one's life, Ustad Ramzi's disorientated manner reminded Gohar Jan of how she herself felt.

Even though it felt strange to her to play for her lone audience, Gohar Jan experienced a familiar joy upon touching, after many days, the well-seasoned wood of the sitar. The fingers of her hand glided over the wooden neck of the instrument, curled around the frets, caressed the strings, and with their touch breathed warmth into the wood. She felt she had recovered a part of herself as her hands held the instrument. Playing it gave her a sense of completeness. As if the coordinates of space were synchronized with the pulse of her emotions, she felt in control of her surroundings. She again felt at home.

As Gohar Jan regarded the silent and lonely man sitting on the carpet, it occurred to her that among the many men who frequented her kotha, Ustad Ramzi was the only one for whom she remained only a voice. It was strange that at the end of her career he was the only person with whom she shared her deep relationship with her art.

The accident of Ustad Ramzi's presence that evening had revealed to Gohar Jan something about herself. She felt indebted to him for making it possible for her to rediscover her art's purpose. It was the first time that, from a feeling of affinity, she felt drawn to him.

After the recital ended, Ustad Ramzi sat for a while with his eyes lowered. He looked up briefly and it seemed he would say something but he silently rose.

Gohar Jan also got up. In a departure from her usual custom she came out to see Ustad Ramzi to the door.

The moneybox where patrons left money had been removed. As Ustad Ramzi tried to inconspicuously put the money in his kerchief and leave it on the side table, Gohar Jan's hand gently touched his.

'Ustad Ramzi,' she said, 'you will be our guest from today.'

For a moment he seemed lost for words. He looked away briefly. Then putting the kerchief with the money on the side table, he looked at Gohar Jan and said, 'It would be improper... otherwise.'

The manner in which Ustad Ramzi had spurned her hospitality and gift rankled in Gohar Jan's heart, but her face did not betray it.

'It shall be as you wish,' Gohar Jan replied with a smile.

The rough manner of the man who had a reputation for never asking anything of anyone was awkward, almost hostile, but not an insult, she told herself. And since it pleased her to have a reason to continue her recitals without receiving men at her kotha, she felt it was best if Ustad Ramzi felt encouraged to visit on his own terms.

Ustad Ramzi bowed his head slightly and went out.

———

On his way home Ustad Ramzi was thoughtful. Gohar Jan had accepted his visit, and given him to understand that he could continue. If in her refusal to accept money there was an acknowledgement of a unique quality to their relationship, he had decisively put an end to it by insisting on making the payment. And yet, he knew that he could not compensate for the privilege he had received from Gohar Jan.

For the first time Ustad Ramzi was assailed by thoughts that questioned his presumptions of himself. He could not rid himself of the feeling that the forthrightness which had guided his conduct in all undertakings, was markedly absent in this affair.

RETURN

Ustad Ramzi's instincts about Imama were right. Kabira brought the news that Imama had started coming to the akhara and had resumed his exercise regime.

Imama sent his challenge to Ustad Ramzi within a month.

Tamami could not believe it when he heard that Ustad Ramzi had finally nominated him to fight. Upon hearing Ustad Ramzi's decision, Imama's clan elders protested that Imama had already defeated Tamami. But Ustad Ramzi contended that it was Imama's choice to fight Tamami. He reminded them that Imama was not bound to fight Tamami according to the established rules of the two clans. He could have disregarded Tamami's challenge since he was not the clan's nominee, so the bout had no significance. Imama's clan elders wished to dispute the point further but Imama put an end to it by declaring he was ready to fight Tamami again.

REGIMEN

Tamami's preparations for the bout began. He was awakened at two in the morning. After saying his prayers, he drank milk in which the flowers of blue lotus and barberries, sandalwood powder, dry endive, myrobalan and green cardamoms had been soaked. He started his sit-ups under the supervision of Kabira and an assistant trainer, and then swung the pair of forty-kilo Indian clubs. Later, he set off on a five-mile run from the akhara to the clock tower and back.

Those who stood along the way or were headed towards the vegetable market in the mornings sometimes caught a glimpse of Tamami leaving or coming back from the run. In the beginning, the bystanders looked at him for a moment or two with indifference and turned away, but after a while, people in the enclave's neighbourhood instinctively began looking out for Tamami in the mornings. His rhythmic, unhurried breathing would reach them long before his shape materialized from the morning mist. They remained silent as he ran past them. Clad in embroidered silken shorts, Tamami ran with his eyes fixed on the ground a few feet ahead of him.

Tamami's mind was preoccupied. He was the official nominee of his clan and Ustad Ramzi's involvement in his training was an acknowledgement of the fact. It had provided him with a chance to prove his worth to his brother. He also wanted to avenge his defeat. Even though Tamami found the training regime gruelling, he endured it with complete submission, never complaining of its unusual harshness. His body, too, kept responding and adjusting to the demands he was making on it by growing stronger.

Often onlookers waited for Tamami in the streets and alleyways, and pointed him out as he came within their range of vision. They no longer looked on with indifference, but with growing interest. Women looked out from the doorways, neighbourhood children ran with him for as long as they could keep up.

A few people began following Tamami to the akhara. Then more came: vendors on their way to the market, carters with hampers who worked in the bazaar, people from the neighbourhood. Some took detours to watch Tamami exercise. As they stood at the open gates of the akhara talking among themselves, Ustad Ramzi watched them silently. Sometimes he caught himself slipping into nostalgia for days when the exhibition grounds used to be full of spectators and rang with their loud cries when the champions grappled.

The number of onlookers swelled daily. After the akhara gate was crowded, a few began climbing up onto the enclosure walls.

Warmed up from the run, Tamami would exercise the muscles of his arms and shoulders, and turn the akhara clay and smooth it. Afterwards he was fed a quarter-kilo of myrobalan preserve and given a breakfast consisting of two kilos of mutton fried in butter.

A short rest was followed by Tamami doing the wheelbarrow exercise with two trainees who lifted his legs for support as he walked on his hands. Then he took a two to three-hour nap.

When he woke up, he was fed a kilo of rabri and handed a mattock to turn the clay of the akhara for an hour. For lunch Tamami had one and a half kilos of roasted meat and after his siesta he again turned the akhara clay and followed that with five hundred push-ups.

The next set of exercises were meant to develop his fighting stamina. A team of five trainees would enter the akhara and attack him: one would secure a lock on his right leg, another would apply a neck lock, one would hold him around the waist and two others would pinion his arms. Tamami grappled with them and when he had tired them out, a fresh team of five trainees would take their place.

On alternate days, the post-breakfast routine was changed and he plied the mattock in the akhara for a half-hour and followed that with push-ups. The moment he finished, Kabira and the assistant trainer would climb onto his back and Tamami would set off on a one-mile run to the bridge that stretched over the canal. He would then smooth the clay in the akhara with two of his trainees straddling his back. Another set of push-ups and a short break later, a fifty-kilo iron ring would be put around Tamami's neck, forty kilo weights would be placed in each hand, and he would be sent on a long run. His trainers made sure that he ran at an even pace until he returned to the akhara. A preparation of gold-foil, pearls and green cardamom in butter would be fed to him upon his return. In cold weather, soup made from five chickens was added to Tamami's regimen.

The rest of the exercise component remained the same with teams of trainees grappling with him at intervals. It had started with two teams, and at the height of his training it progressed to four teams of five trainees each. Tamami grappled with them, and even when he was exhausted, sparred with them for as long as he could hold up.

The exercises ended a few hours after sunset, and then for two hours, Tamami's body was massaged with mustard oil by the trainees to release the tension in the muscles and soothe his nerves.

———

The spectators cheered Tamami daily. Awed by Tamami's strength, they applauded him as he destroyed the combined attack of several trainees. They egged him on, and booed the trainees who dropped out after sparring with Tamami.

Later, when they discussed these grappling sessions before others, they often exaggerated the number of trainees Tamami fought. When Tamami did his pushups, they remarked on the pooling of sweat from his body that traced the outlines of his form on the ground. When he began his leg-squats, they made bets on how many more he would do during that session. The trainees made bets among themselves to see who would last longest against Tamami.

Returning from his run one day, Tamami noticed Imama and other members of his clan standing at one end of the exhibition grounds. They had come to watch how his preparations were progressing. They regarded him intently for some time and left.

———

Tamami grew both heavier and wider in the chest and shoulders. Covered in sweat and clay, his skin shone with the vigour of youth. His intense and punishing training regime was not only transforming his physique, it was also building up a fierce rage inside him. Pain assailed every nerve in his body, but he gave no indication that he felt it, as he stared fixedly at the wall of the enclosure while exercising. The presence of the spectators and their encouragement kept Tamami going from one routine to the next. The thought that after winning the bout he would have an undeniable claim on the title made every sacrifice worthwhile for him.

During one grappling session, Tamami was feeling overwhelmed by the fresh trainees, when he heard the crowd jeering. Instilled with a new vigour, he attacked the trainees, hitting them on their temples and shoulders.

The trainers stopped the session but the same thing happened again a few days later. The trainees complained to Kabira who suggested that Ustad Ramzi allow some light modification in the grappling session so that Tamami was not exhausted and violent at the end. Ustad Ramzi overruled him and maintained the same routines, instructing Tamami to check his violence.

———

Promoter Gulab Deen returned from organizing exhibition bouts upcountry and at Ustad Ramzi's invitation came to see Tamami grapple with the trainees. He was surprised to see people crowding the akhara gate and sitting astride the walls. In the eyes and faces of those assembled there, the promoter read something that astonished him. They were not there as mere spectators to see the grappling match and its outcome. They had come to watch Tamami; they seemed involved in his life. Gulab Deen had never witnessed such popular interest in a pahalwan.

Later, when he saw Tamami in the akhara, he could not recognize him as the pahalwan he had seen a few months ago.

'What do you say, Gulab Deen?' Ustad Ramzi asked.

'This isn't the Tamami I knew!' promoter Gulab Deen exclaimed. 'People will come when he fights,' he muttered. 'Yes, they will come.'

Ustad Ramzi did not comment. Tamami's physical development had surprised him too.

Tamami had weighed so little at birth that the elders decided he did not have the frame or constitution of a pahalwan. In the beginning his interests lay outside the akhara. Stray kittens were attracted to him by instinct, and pye-dogs followed him around. He spent his time painstakingly teaching fledgling parrots to mimic speech. And at school, neither birching nor the promise of reward could turn his attention to studies. Ustad Ramzi had given up his hopes for him, until at the age of seventeen Tamami developed an interest in the akhara. Ustad Ramzi told himself it was a passing fancy. Despite a certain fickleness that remained in his manner, Tamami persevered and his body filled out from the rigours of exercise.

Gulab Deen often came to the akhara and Tamami learned from him that the two exhibition bouts he had organized upcountry were well-attended and the pahalwans paid good money. Things were not looking quite as bleak for the pahalwans because of Gulab Deen's efforts.

One day a pahalwan named Sher Ali from upcountry accompanied Gulab Deen to Ustad Ramzi's enclosure. Gulab Deen had been promoting him in exhibition bouts. Although young and not representative of any clan, Sher Ali was more experienced than many trainees from the two wrestling clans. After Tamami had sparred with the trainees Sher Ali entered the akhara.

Ustad Ramzi saw Tamami grapple with him for a few minutes. The thought occurred to him that Tamami had missed a few opportunities for takedown, before he realized that Tamami was deliberately prolonging their engagement. The trainees who had not understood it became restless wondering why Tamami was unable to

bring down Sher Ali. Another few minutes passed before Tamami finally took down Sher Ali.

'What were you trying to show others? That Sher
Ali is your match?' Ustad Ramzi said to Tamami after
Gulab Deen had left.

'No Ustad... I was just trying to see what he knew.'
Tamami smiled sheepishly.

'Don't waste time playing with your opponents,' Ustad
Ramzi said.

————

When Gulab Deen called on Ustad Ramzi with a gift
of fermented tobacco, he said, 'Ustad Ramzi, I would
like to do something for Tamami. He has not fought an
exhibition bout since he started his training. You know
it helps in promoting a pahalwan's name.'

Ustad Ramzi stared ahead at the trainees cleaning
up the akhara.

'If you will give me permission I will organize an
exhibition bout for Tamami.'

'With whom?' Ustad Ramzi turned to him.

'With Sher Ali.'

'Sher Ali? The one who sparred with Tamami the
other day?'

'Yes, Ustad,' Gulab Deen answered. 'He is young and
strong. You have seen him fight.' Ustad Ramzi remained

silent for a moment, then said, 'Tamami is under preparation for something more important. Why don't you organize a bout for one of the trainees? It would give them something to look forward to.'

'It will be a good opportunity for publicity, Ustad. If Tamami fights with Sher Ali, and it's a tie, more people will come to watch him when...'

'A tie!' Ustad Ramzi rose angrily before Gulab Deen could finish. 'You know well our clan never participated in fixed fights. Not even for exhibition bouts. Nor did we fight those who did. That was the only way to make sure nobody could ever claim a pahalwan from our clan won by prearrangement.'

'The money will pay for the trainees' training...' Gulab Deen said.

'We don't need the money! If one has the determination to be a pahalwan, he can build his constitution on a diet of just one almond a day.'

'Why don't you discuss this with Tamami?'

'I know his answer. He will refuse,' Ustad Ramzi said. Suddenly a suspicion entered his mind.

'Did you speak to Tamami about it?' he asked.

'He asked me to talk to you first,' Gulab Deen replied.

What the promoter said made it clear that Tamami had an understanding with Gulab Deen.

That Tamami should fall so low as to agree to a fixed

fight enraged Ustad Ramzi. He felt vexed at him also because it was his prerogative alone to discuss all issues related to Tamami's bouts with others. He was furious at Gulab Deen's temerity in approaching him with an offer for a fixed fight for Tamami.

Ustad Ramzi told the promoter that he would give him an answer in a few days.

———

The next morning Tamami was turning the akhara clay when Ustad Ramzi came out of his room. Most of the spectators had left, but the trainees were present. Tamami noticed the frown on Ustad Ramzi's face and felt a vague unease. He had been wondering what Ustad Ramzi would decide about the exhibition bout. Gulab Deen had not disclosed his plans, but he had advised him on several occasions not to overwhelm his opponents too quickly. He explained that people felt encouraged to come to bouts when they expected to witness a drawn-out fight; that he always made this a condition for the exhibition bouts organized by him upcountry. He knew it went against the spirit and tradition of the art, which aimed at defeating the opponent in the shortest possible time, but in the absence of any patrons and benefactors it was the only way to keep people's interest alive in wrestling bouts and provide a livelihood for the pahalwans.

Ustad Ramzi avoided mentioning the fixed fight, but he reproved Tamami before everyone for discussing the organization of a challenge bout with Gulab Deen without first consulting him. Tamami felt anger at being censured before everyone.

'So what if I fight Sher Ali, Ustad?' he said heatedly. It was the first time he had argued with Ustad Ramzi. He had not learned of the arrangement the promoter had proposed to Ustad Ramzi.

'No.' Ustad Ramzi replied in a firm voice. 'He is not your match.'

'If he challenges me, I want to fight him!' Tamami said raising his voice. The feeling that he was being treated unfairly annoyed him. His grip tightened over the handle of the mattock with which he had been turning the akhara clay.

'It is decided!' Ustad Ramzi shouted. 'If you wish otherwise, you can have Gulab Deen arrange your affairs. I will withdraw!' His tone became more grating with each syllable.

Tamami was afraid that Ustad Ramzi might recall his nomination for the challenge bout with Imama. He did not wish to lose the trust that Ustad Ramzi had recently reposed in him. His anxiety eroded his confidence, and his deep-rooted sense of inadequacy made him apprehensive.

'No, Ustad, I won't fight Sher Ali,' Tamami's voice shook and the smooth handle of the mattock felt slippery in his hands. 'I won't give you cause for complaint again.' The expression on Ustad Ramzi's face hardened. Two days later, when the promoter returned, Ustad Ramzi sent for Tamami. Ustad Ramzi looked at Tamami as he entered his quarters and sat down. He turned to Gulab Deen and said, 'Tamami wants to tell you something.' Tamami had guessed what Ustad Ramzi wanted. 'I have decided not to fight Sher Ali,' Tamami said to Gulab Deen slowly with lowered eyes. The promoter seemed to happily accept his decision. He took his leave shortly afterwards and the two brothers sat silently for a few minutes without exchanging a word. Tamami stared fixedly at the ground. 'Do you have anything to say?' Ustad Ramzi finally asked. 'No,' Tamami said, and left the room.

LOSS

Gohar Jan had not seen Maulvi Hidayatullah, the imam of the local mosque, in many weeks. When she learned from the trinket-seller, Shukran, that he had passed away, she felt deeply grieved. In the thirty odd years that Maulvi Hidayatullah had been the imam, she never found his manner towards her at all condescending, or in any way disparaging. He could not have approved of her life; yet whenever he had started a collection, whether it was to put a new roof on the main assembly hall, to extend the left wing, or do other renovations, he never refused her assistance. He had never hidden it from his congregation when she had donated money for the white-wash and repairs of the mosque.

The trinket-seller also told Gohar Jan that after Hidayatullah, his protégé, Yameen, had been appointed as the new imam.

'Yameen?' Gohar Jan said. She remembered him as a boy who often visited the tawaifs' enclave when food offerings for the saints were distributed to commemorate them.

'He had been growing his beard in anticipation of this day...' Shukran said. 'The old maulvi was a good soul, God knows. But Yameen! The other day it was very hot and I went in to wash my face at the ablution post when he came out and started shouting at me, "The water's only for making ablutions. You should not come here again..." The old maulvi's winding sheets are not soiled yet, and Yameen has already become the Almighty. Now that the month of Ramzaan is here, he is going around the kothas collecting penance money from those who do not fast.'

As Banday Ali entered the living room Gohar Jan asked him to bring the bundle of old clothes she had set aside for Shukran.

'Why did you shut down the kotha, Gohar Jan?' Shukran asked. 'If I had not run into your servant girl the other day, I would never have found out. In such silence, as if the whole affair was nothing. Who could have thought! And you let Malka fly away too. At least you should have made her pay for all the expenses you incurred in feeding and clothing her. If you had only let me know I would have brought ten men who'd have paid all that and more for her.'

Gohar Jan was saved from answering when Banday Ali brought in the bundle of clothes and gave it to Shukran.

'May God visit his mercies upon you, Gohar Jan! May all calamities be warded off from the head of you and yours!' Shukran said as she caressed the bundle of clothes.

Gohar Jan asked Banday Ali to see to it that the servant girl brought Shukran something to eat with her tea, and got up and left the room.

RAGE

Experienced pahalwans occasionally tested how well a young champion remembered his skills when he was exhausted. On one occasion Tamami was challenged by a respected pahalwan of his clan soon after finishing his last grappling session with the trainees.

'Let us see what you have to show!' he called out, stepping up to Tamami.

Nodding in response, Tamami faced him.

After sparring for a few moments, the old pahalwan applied a drag to trip Tamami onto his back. His push triggered inside Tamami an impulse to strike back. He caught his opponent around the shoulders, with a violent shove threw him onto his back, and pinned him down by sitting on his chest.

Tamami instantly realized that humiliating the old pahalwan in this manner was offensive and wrong. When a junior pahalwan pinned down a senior adversary during a sparring session, he placed his hand lightly on his chest.

Tamami hastily got up and apologized to the old pahalwan.

His opponent said nothing.

Ustad Ramzi had watched the spectacle in silence.

Later, when Kabira asked Tamami about it, he could not explain why he acted with such unbridled rage. The fury that had been building up inside him had come out instinctively. He had often felt such impulses during recent grappling sessions, but the violence of his counter-manoeuvres was dissipated by the combined force of trainees attacking him simultaneously. Still, two trainees had dislocated their shoulders in the last few weeks.

———

The news of Tamami's violence in the akhara was questioned by the clan elders.

Ustad Ramzi had felt uneasy when Tamami sat on the old pahalwan's chest, but he did not reprimand Tamami. The incident was an expression of Tamami's training and not contrary to its focus. Ustad Ramzi designed Tamami's exercise routines with an emphasis on sub-duing the adversary by force. They were based on his own estimation of Tamami's ability.

Ustad Ramzi could not share his reasons with any-one. He told himself there would be time to correct it once Imama's challenge had been thwarted. Yet, in his heart something bothered him.

When Kabira came by later that day and asked to have a word with him in private, Ustad Ramzi called him into his living quarters.

'What do you say about Tamami's regime of exercises, Ramzi?' Kabira came straight to the point. 'Now that he is doing well, shouldn't you taper them down a little? His body needs some suppleness, too.'

'If he were unable to endure it, his body would not grow in size with every passing week,' Ustad Ramzi answered evasively. 'He is preparing to defend the clan's title. You know what happened the last time he fought Imama. We cannot take any chances.'

It was true that Tamami's body continued to grow and without flinching he performed the new, harder tasks added to his routines.

Kabira regarded Ustad Ramzi intently as if he won-dered whether Ustad Ramzi himself understood what he had said.

'Ustad Ramzi,' Kabira said, 'I've known Tamami since childhood. What I see in his eyes I've never seen before. This exercise regimen is too harsh. Moderate it a little. Allow him a reprieve.'

Ustad Ramzi was made uncomfortable by Kabira's words.

'Strength may be mistaken, but the body never lies. I will taper down his exercises once the growth of his body is settled.'

'You can see that he is feeling the strain.'

'In that case he can speak for himself.'

'You know he would never say a word to you about it. He wants your approval.'

Ustad Ramzi made no answer.

Their conversation ended there and Kabira left.

———

Kabira saw no reprieve in Tamami's exercise routine in the days that followed. He did not accost Ustad Ramzi again. But one day he had a long talk with Tamami, and tried to persuade him to ask Ustad Ramzi himself to reduce his exercise load. Exhausted and under brutal strain, Tamami broke into tears from the affection and friendly concern he heard in Kabira's words. Yet, he refused to ask Ustad Ramzi for a relaxation of his schedule and persevered with it.

RAINS

Heavy rains fell on the inner city after a long dry spell, washing away the layers of limestone paint from the old buildings, exposing more patches of their brickwork. Water, which had united elements in the process of construction, now aided disintegration, allowing decay to make deeper inroads into the edifices. New cracks formed in the aged roofs and old walls. The groundwater rose. The old sewers overflowed and puddles of rainwater formed in the alleyways.

After many complaints were made, the municipal staff made preliminary rounds to check the situation and assess the damage in the tawaifs' enclave, but in their sprawling, chaotic order of priorities the neighbourhood had lost its place. They did not return to make any repairs or drain the water.

The suffocating humidity had ended with the rains, however, and Gohar Jan felt relieved since it made things a little more bearable.

One of the awnings of the Music Room suddenly fell one night. Upon hearing the noise Gohar Jan opened the door to the unlit room and saw the dust from the rubble clouding the moonlight in the room. Disturbed in his sleep by the noise, Banday Ali followed her into the room to investigate its source.

Fortunately, the alley was deserted at that late hour, and nobody had been hurt by the falling debris. By afternoon the following day Gohar Jan had the fallen awning removed and asked Banday Ali to find someone to make the repairs.

Banday Ali summoned a mason who inspected the other awnings and found that they, too, had developed cracks. The awnings had to be repaired before the next spell of rain. Gohar Jan refused to go ahead with the repairs when the mason told her that the work would go on for a fortnight. She told Banday Ali that removing the carpets, and storing away and rearranging the furniture in rooms so that repairs could be made, would throw the whole place into disorder. She would attend to the repairs a few months later when she had the energy to organize everything.

Uncharacteristically, Banday Ali did not try to persuade her to carry out the repairs. It was the second time in recent days that he had not questioned her reasons for a decision. When Gohar Jan had announced to him that she had given up her morning riyazat, Banday Ali had similarly remained quiet.

It had been Gohar Jan's routine for decades to get up before dawn. After saying her morning prayers, she would perform the riyazat until sunlight scaled down the courtyard walls and it was time for Banday Ali to bring her tea.

When she had fallen sick and Banday Ali had asked her to rest, she had told him, 'If I give up the riyazat I will not find the strength to carry on with my life.' Recently she had been ill again. When Banday Ali again insisted that she could not cope with the exertion of both her morning riyazat and the evening recital she held for Ustad Ramzi, Gohar Jan gave up her morning ritual instead of asking Ustad Ramzi to end his visits.

Banday Ali's silence at the news had forced Gohar Jan to say, 'You always asked me to rest. I have finally decided to take your advice.'

But Gohar Jan was conscious that she had compromised a principle of her life. She could not help it. She did not wish anything to intrude on or hinder her evening recital. The threat of its disruption by repairs to the room again made her conscious of how much she cherished those moments. And yet she could not bring herself to share her reasons with Banday Ali.

DEFENDER

On Gulab Deen's advice Ustad Ramzi paid for an advertisement in the newspaper and the whole city learned that Ustad Ramzi's younger brother would be defending the title of Ustad-e-Zaman for his clan.

Tamami stopped his exercises two days before the fight to allow his body some rest to make it more flexible.

The trainees spent these days marking the stalls for the spectators, and turning and smoothing the clay in the newly made akhara in the exhibition grounds. The night before the bout, it was sprinkled with rose water. Tamami and Imama had separately visited the place the previous evening and had been satisfied with the softness of the clay.

The lights in the trainee quarters were extinguished and the words of *ayat-e-karima* with which Prophet Yunus had sought deliverance in the darkness of the leviathan's belly were recited on each almond for up to five thousand and one hundred times. Early in the morning a special preparation of sardai made from these almonds was fed to Tamami.

The promoter brought along a photographer who took a number of photographs of Tamami with Gulab Deen. Trainees prevailed on Ustad Ramzi, too, to have one taken with his brother.

A clan elder sent two sacks of almonds for the akhara and a turban of braided silk with a cash gift for Tamami.

Pitchers of sardai were sent from Imama's akhara to the exhibition grounds for the spectators.

People had begun turning out since early morning to secure a good spot. They filled the stalls of the exhibition ground hours before the bout. The walls of the adjoining alleys were also lined with people, who had climbed up there when they could not find a better view. Some had managed to get inside the exhibition grounds through one of the loosely guarded entrances. Gulab Deen bitterly complained that he had been cheated out of their ticket money.

Tamami was being massaged by three trainees. He kept lying on his belly, his head turned to one side.

It occurred to Tamami that if he won against Imama, he would have beaten the man who very nearly defeated Ustad Ramzi – the man who would certainly defeat Ustad Ramzi if they were to fight again. Tamami realized it was he who was defending the title of Ustad-e-Zaman. Did that not mean that in all fairness it belonged to him? Would Ustad Ramzi not see that and bow out in his favour?

Tamami could read no answer in the eyes of Ustad Ramzi as he fumed Tamami's fighter's belt and turban with an incense burner.

A distant beating of the dhol was heard in the alleys. It signalled that Imama was on his way to the akhara.

Tamami got up from the massage bench.

Ustad Ramzi tied the turban on Tamami's head.

Concerned that his clan should not be seen to be making the least show of vanity at that important moment, Ustad Ramzi instructed Kabira to ensure that Tamami entered the akhara before Imama. He also told him to make sure the excited trainees did not make any disparaging comments about Imama or his clan.

Even as Ustad Ramzi gave his last instructions, the trainees picked up Tamami on their shoulders and headed out of the akhara to the exhibition grounds.

———

As happened with true champions, when Tamami stepped into the akhara his body seemed to have been transformed and become larger in anticipation of the fight.

Ustad Ramzi saw Imama's eyes flash with jealousy when Tamami removed the embroidered coverlet from his body. Ustad Ramzi realized Imama must have been reminded of his crippled son – now sitting on the sidelines.

When Ustad Ramzi saw the contestants approach the judge to seek permission to begin, he felt relieved that his struggle to see Tamami through that stage was over. His clan would soon be delivered of Imama's challenge. The next step for him would be to help Tamami choose someone among his trainees as his protégé and prepare a schedule to guide him through the initial phase of his training. Tamami could take over his supervision from there. The clan's defence would then become fully impregnable.

Ustad Ramzi saw Imama bend down. He picked up the akhara clay and rubbed it over Tamami's body as a token of admiration by a senior pahalwan towards his adversary. By rubbing Tamami's body with clay to allow for better grip during holds, Imama had implied he expected it to be a long, drawn-out encounter and not one that would end with a few moves. It was a gesture of goodwill and sportsmanship, and it was not lost on the trainees of the two clans who cheered the contestants. The pahalwans embraced, stepped back, and did quick leg-squats to flex their muscles.

It seemed to Ustad Ramzi that through the force of his will he had perpetuated the glory of his clan to which his life had been dedicated. Immersed in these thoughts, he almost missed Imama's opening move.

———

Tamami had broken Imama's hold with just a shrug of his upper body. They faced each other again. In that brief interlude, as Imama was preparing for the next move, some trainees from Imama's clan began shouting:

'Throw him down, Imama!'

'Show him once more who the true champion is!'

Tamami's eyes met Ustad Ramzi's. He thought he saw a sneer on Ustad Ramzi's face. Perhaps Ustad Ramzi wondered if he would try to prolong the fight. Tamami's body became tense and the expression on his face hardened. His eyes were fixed on Imama's. He resolved to show his brother how quickly he could eliminate his adversary.

At that moment he considered that if he gave the fight to Imama it would open the way for him to wrest the title from him later, *after* Imama had vanquished Ustad Ramzi. He would not have to be indebted to Ustad Ramzi for withdrawing in his favour. Shocked at the baseness of his thoughts, Tamami violently shook his head.

'Throw him down, Imama! Throw him down!' the chorus continued.

The trainees from Ustad Ramzi's clan now answered:

'Don't show him any mercy, Tamami, if you are your mother's son!'

'Kill the rat now, Tamami! Enough of playing with him!'

Imama's clan was to blame for starting the shouting match, but Ustad Ramzi was angered by this breakdown of discipline among the trainees of his clan. He shouted at them to shut up.

The thought of losing to Imama again entered Tamami's mind. He tried to drive the thought away. Imama lurched forward to attack. Tamami hit out as a sudden surge of power filled his body.

Imama reeled and fell, struck on his left temple by Tamami's powerful forearm. People roared with excitement, but the next moment everyone fell quiet. Imama had rolled over and become still.

No one sitting around the akhara moved. Only those standing in the back rows surged forward to see what had happened. Someone from Imama's clan shouted, calling for a doctor. As Tamami moved towards him, he was held back by Kabira.

As the members of Ustad Imama's clan began pouring into the akhara, Kabira signalled to the trainees, who quickly circled Tamami and took him away to a safe distance.

———

'Imama is dead!' Ustad Ramzi muttered to himself in disbelief.

The pahalwan's corpse was carried away to the hospital for a post-mortem after the doctor confirmed his death. A couple of hours after the incident, the police arrived to record the witnesses' statements. Tamami was deposed before a magistrate. Ustad Ramzi accompanied him to the court for the deposition. After returning to his quarters Tamami locked himself in his room. Ustad Ramzi sent everyone away.

Later in the evening he called on the elders of Imama's clan. The initial post-mortem report identified brain haemorrhage as the cause of death.

Retiring to his quarters late at night, Ustad Ramzi hesitated as he passed Tamami's door. He almost knocked but something held him back.

———

For several days after Imama's death, Tamami did not attend the akhara. He remained closeted in his room. When a week had passed, Kabira tried to persuade him to get back to his routine in the akhara. Tamami refused.

When he started attending the akhara at Kabira's insistence, Tamami exercised alone. He refused the massage and later, when he started grappling, on occasions he abruptly left the akhara. Ustad Ramzi sent him to their ancestral village to rest for a month.

He also wanted to shield Tamami from the vicious comments that were being made concerning Imama's death and his role in it.

'I knew that something would happen the day I saw Tamami sit on his trainer's chest!'

'They say once they have tasted blood, they develop a liking for it.'

'It was Ustad Ramzi's covetousness for his title that killed Imama.'

'He attended Imama's burial too – went there to make sure they bury him deep!'

'Who would now challenge Ustad Ramzi after witnessing the manner in which Tamami killed Imama?'

Ustad Ramzi told himself that tongues had wagged against him in the past, too; that he must not pay any heed to the comments. But it made him uneasy that more than Tamami, these barbs targeted him.

DONATION

Gohar Jan had heard that the mosque's roof was damaged by the rains and a collection had been started for the repairs. She planned to send money for the repairs as she had always done, but something about the trinketseller Shukran's report on the young maulvi made her reconsider her decision.

In the evening as Ustad Ramzi was leaving the kotha after the recital she brought an envelope to him and said, 'I would like to ask a favour of you... Please give it to Maulvi Yameen for repairs to the mosque roof.'

As Ustad Ramzi took the money, Gohar Jan said, 'And please do not mention who sent it.'

She saw Ustad Ramzi hesitate. He looked uncomfortable for a moment. But he took the envelope and after counting the money put it away in his kurta pocket.

As Ustad Ramzi left, Gohar Jan regretted asking him to deliver the money. She told herself she should have found another means of sending the money.

Ustad Ramzi's reluctance had hurt her. She recalled his insisting on paying for the recitals after the kotha's closure, and felt that the graciousness that impelled people to accept and grant small kindnesses had no place in Ustad Ramzi's heart. For the first time it also occurred to her that it gave him a certain privilege in his relationships: he could neither be dismissed as a stranger nor held to any commitment to anyone.

The thought made her unhappy, but she could not help feeling sorry for Ustad Ramzi at the same time.

———

Ustad Ramzi was vexed with himself. He had unwittingly embroiled himself in a business that had nothing to do with him. He regretted giving his consent so hastily to Gohar Jan, but it was too late to refuse. The realization that Gohar Jan had accepted his visits to the kotha on his own terms had been a source of consolation to him. It troubled him now that she had felt free to make a change in their arrangement.

On the way to the mosque, Ustad Ramzi thought about the ethical value of what he had accepted to do for Gohar Jan. If Gohar Jan had any apprehensions that her donation would be rejected, she should not have sent it anonymously by his hand. And if Maulvi Yameen wished to refuse a donation on principle, why must he pass it off as from someone else?

Ustad Ramzi was further troubled when at the mosque Yameen thanked him profusely for the money. Ustad Ramzi told him that it was an anonymous donation. As Yameen continued to thank him, Ustad Ramzi felt that perhaps Yameen thought he was refusing to acknowledge the donation out of religious modesty. He felt it improper that he should receive credit for someone else's charity.

Ustad Ramzi finally told Maulvi Yameen that the money came from Gohar Jan who wished to remain anonymous.

TAINT

Gohar Jan had returned from a visit to a neighbouring kotha when she heard a knock on the door. Answering it, she found the visitor had already climbed down a few steps. She could not make out his face on the dark stairwell.

'Who is it?' Gohar Jan asked.

'Maulvi Yameen from the mosque.'

'Oh, Yameen,' she looked closely. Gohar Jan had not seen him for some years.

'How fast children grow up... Come inside, boy... Poor Maulvi Hidayatullah... I found out about his passing away much later...'

'I am in a bit of a hurry,' Maulvi Yameen said. 'I have to go to a few other places before the Asr prayers.'

'It does not look nice talking standing outside like this, child. If you are in a hurry we could send someone to the mosque tomorrow,' she said.

'All right, I will come in,' he quickly replied. 'But only for a minute.'

She could barely recognize him with his beard.

Gohar Jan showed him into the veranda. Yameen avoided eye contact with her.

'What is it about?' she asked, once he had sat down on one of the chairs near the potted palms.

'I came to tell you…about the money you sent. The repair work has begun.'

'I am glad to hear that,' Gohar Jan said.

Ustad Ramzi had not been discreet, she realized.

Maulvi Yameen looked away again. She sensed restraint in his manner and wondered about its reason.

'There is something about which I… it's about your donation…' he finally said, and stopped again. 'I have to write a receipt… for amounts over one hundred rupees. At the end of the month, the mosque committee looks at the receipt books. There is a small problem. A small thing, but… someone might… they might not like the idea of… you should not think… what I mean to say is that they might object. They can object. They might blame the person who accepted it… In this case I would be held responsible. But the repairs were needed urgently.

For me, the mosque and the comfort of the worshippers come first. Of course, if you would like your donation to be returned…

'I can arrange for it. It may take a little time, but it can be arranged.'

Gohar Jan found herself unprepared for such presumption and effrontery. She had done something that needed to be done without being asked, and as far as she was concerned, the matter had ended there. But not only was she being reminded that her charity was tainted, she was being humiliated as well.

The sudden, impulsive glare of anger died however, even as it flashed in her blood. Seeing the man seated before her, Gohar Jan only felt a sense of loss for the child she had known. The whole thing was so contemptible that she felt the matter had absolutely no relevance or connection to her.

'I would not care for the receipt. I do not have any use for it,' she said calmly. 'You can say it was an anonymous donation. I would prefer it to be that way, too. Nobody else has to know, and the matter of the receipt would not even arise.'

Gohar Jan now wondered if Yameen had visited the kotha because he did not like the idea of Banday Ali or somebody else calling at the mosque at her behest again.

'Only if it is all right with you...' Maulvi Yameen said, avoiding her eyes. 'I will go now.'

When she said nothing, he quietly got up and left.

Gohar Jan wistfully thought of the old Maulvi Hidayatullah again and felt a strange sense of loss.

The burdensome, depressing feeling that she had felt in Maulvi Yameen's presence and which had momentarily lifted as he had walked away, returned. It was not so much the changing times that troubled her, but the worst they seemed to bring out in people.

———

When Ustad Ramzi next visited Gohar Jan he brought up the subject of the donation and mentioned that he had told Maulvi Yameen who had sent the money.

'He thought it was from me,' Ustad Ramzi continued. 'In the past, too, I know you had helped the mosque on a number of occasions. I saw no reason why your name should not be acknowledged.'

'Thank you for delivering the donation for me,' Gohar Jan said. 'It was for the best. Please think no more about it.'

As Gohar Jan reached for the sitar, Ustad Ramzi no longer felt sure about the propriety of what he had done.

DREAD

Powerful and conflicting emotions always made Tamami take the avenue of self-reproach whenever he attempted to reflect on the events of that fateful day when Imama was felled by his hand. He never stopped thinking about that moment. For weeks afterwards, he shrank from human touch.

Tamami could still feel the sensation of his forearm hitting Imama's skull. He kept recalling that moment of contact and sensing it in the nerves of his forearm. When he resumed grappling in the akhara, he would pull away violently if a trainee caught his right forearm. The time he had spent in the village away from the akhara hardly calmed his nerves.

No new challengers came forward to contest Ustad Ramzi's title in the meanwhile. But Tamami resumed his training regime to ensure that Ustad Ramzi did not find him remiss in his duties.

His desire to acquire the title of Ustad-e-Zaman had remained alive in him although Ustad Ramzi had not mentioned anything about it since the day Imama died.

Tamami knew that Imama's death was behind the pahalwans' refusal to challenge Ustad Ramzi. He was not deaf to what others said about his fight with Imama. A dread sometimes seized him that no one would ever challenge Ustad Ramzi again. As the passing days re-inforced this fear in his mind, his strenuous schedule seemed increasingly oppressive and punishing.

He suffered in equal measure from the unspoken stigma of being a murderer and the physical pain of the exercises which increasingly seemed futile to him. A dark void tested Tamami's will. When he stepped into the akhara he felt conscious of a presence that bore down and suffocated him. Slowly that presence acquired a face. As he recognized the face as Ustad Ramzi's, base thoughts took hold in Tamami's mind once more.

He began to neglect his akhara duties again.

———

Ustad Ramzi was alone in the akhara in the early hours one morning. An earthy, spicy fragrance rose from the clay that was moist with dew. When he looked towards Tamami's room he saw that its windows were still dark. The dilapidated building which stood at the periphery of the akhara shielded the trainees' quarters in the westerly building from his view. However, he could not see any one of them in the akhara. Two trainees had stopped coming altogether in the last few weeks. Later, Ustad Ramzi discovered they had joined Imama's clan. He felt keenly that Tamami's behaviour was having an adverse effect on the trainees.

These developments convinced Ustad Ramzi that Tamami symbolized everything that had gone wrong with his life. Whenever something was expected of Tamami, or worse, when something was entrusted to him, disaster followed. Ustad Ramzi was reminded of those instances every time he looked at his brother.

PACT

Some days later, Tamami received a message that Gulab Deen wished to discuss something important privately with him.

'I know that Imama's death was an accident and what people are saying is false, but there is no stopping their tongues,' Gulab Deen said when they got together. 'They say that Tamami has become a killer. Nobody fights a pahalwan with such a reputation. In these circumstances, a pahalwan who agrees to a bout with you should be shown a little respect. Without an arrangement you would not get a fight.'

Tamami listened in silence.

'Sher Ali is still willing to fight,' Gulab Deen said. 'But only if you draw out the fight a little, so that the spectators get a chance to enjoy the pahalwans' engagement.'

Tamami became thoughtful. Gulab Deen cautioned him, 'Ustad Ramzi must not learn about this arrangement. If he had meant to get you a challenger himself, he would not have objected to your fighting Sher Ali. Ustad Ramzi wants to take his title to his grave, I'm sure.

'You mustn't overlook another thing which is to your advantage. If you prolong the fight, you will get rid of the blemish and encourage more pahalwans to try their luck by challenging you. Once your bout with Imama is forgotten, you can issue an open challenge. When you have defeated the challengers, there will be no question as to who must have the title of Ustad-e-Zaman!'

———

Tamami did not wish to offend his brother so he asked Kabira to mention Gulab Deen's idea of an exhibition bout to Ustad Ramzi to see how he would react.

Ustad Ramzi did not comment when Kabira communicated the message, thereby giving the idea his tacit approval.

Tamami was relieved at first. He finally had the freedom to act according to his own wishes and to develop his own exercise regime.

But, as the days passed, Tamami felt that Ustad Ramzi was ignoring everything related to his preparation for the fight. He felt that Ustad Ramzi had been interested in his training only because his own title was at stake. Now Ustad Ramzi did not express interest because Tamami fought for his own name. His older brother left him alone because he did not wish to be part of a process that could ultimately lead to his relinquishing his title.

The brothers seldom spoke, unless it was about something related to the akhara or the trainees. They almost never exchanged any words in private. Ustad Ramzi felt easier addressing Tamami when others were present. Tamami also seemed to prefer it, and answered with less awkwardness and inhibition. The distance between them grew.

DEFIANCE

During the exhibition bout Ustad Ramzi observed Tamami prolonging the fight with Sher Ali. He angrily left the akhara when he realized Tamami was doing something which he had expressly forbidden him to do. The trainees followed him. Gulab Deen was worried when he saw Ustad Ramzi leave, but when Tamami ignored Ustad Ramzi's departure and continued with the bout, Gulab Deen did not try to call him back. Tamami won the fight.

There were many spectators. Promoter Gulab Deen was overjoyed.

'I told you,' he said to Tamami after the fight. 'Someone who has the art to pin down his opponent within a minute has the art to delay it for a half-hour, too.

A half-hour only. A half-hour is all I ask. You saw for yourself. Nobody complained. Everyone will come again.'

Gulab Deen kept Tamami up late talking about the great things that he had planned for him. He told Tamami not to worry about anyone or anything.

When Tamami returned to the akhara, he was satisfied by the decision he had made independently of his brother. For the first time in his life, he had defied Ustad Ramzi and his brother had been unable to do anything.

When Tamami emerged from his quarter the next morning and greeted his brother, Ustad Ramzi did not return his greeting. Tamami felt the trainees also avoided him. Kabira told him that Ustad Ramzi had taken charge of the trainees again.

Kabira told him that the previous night, after Ustad Ramzi returned from the exhibition bout, he had overheard the trainees talking about the variety of holds and locks they had witnessed in Tamami's fight with Sher Ali. He had been furious.

'A pahalwan does not sell his body!' Ustad Ramzi had shouted angrily. 'Tamami brought disgrace to the clan by fighting a fixed bout with Sher Ali.'

Everyone was silenced by Ustad Ramzi's outburst, Kabira told Tamami. Ustad Ramzi remained irritable and short-tempered the rest of the evening and forbade the trainees from having anything to do with Tamami.

Tamami sat around in the akhara, looking around and pondering what he must do. When Kabira asked him when he would start his exercises, Tamami told him that he was taking a day of rest. He left the akhara and spent the day with friends in the neighbourhood.

When Tamami returned, Ustad Ramzi had retired to his room, the trainees had gone to their quarters and Kabira had also left. Except for the old enclosure attendant, there was no one in the akhara. Standing there, Tamami felt lonelier and more powerless than he had ever felt in his life.

RESOLVE

Tamami came to the akhara an hour late one day. This happened again a few days later. Ustad Ramzi was told that Tamami had modified his old exercise regime. After a few weeks, at his own initiative, Tamami further reduced it. Then he began to come home late at night. He slept longer and showed up later and later for the morning exercises. He finished the training sessions early, too.

It was whispered among the trainees that Tamami was taking drugs.

One evening Tamami returned later than usual and went to sleep. The room was left unlatched from inside and the light was on. Unable to contain himself any longer, Ustad Ramzi searched the room and found a small paper packet that contained the drug residue.

This was grim confirmation of all the rumours that had been flying around. He felt more devastated than if he had found Tamami lying dead.

The trainees noticed that Tamami took longer rests, then quit in the middle of the exercises. Ustad Ramzi saw pahalwans leaving the akhara whispering among themselves.

One afternoon Tamami woke up late and went out. The trainees who were busily discussing these events in the courtyard silently dispersed when Ustad Ramzi stepped out of his quarters.

Tamami had not yet returned to the akhara in the evening when Ustad Ramzi gave a lock to the attendant and asked him to lock the gate of the enclosure. After the gate was locked, he took the key from the attendant.

'It shall remain locked tonight,' he said.

The attendant looked puzzled and said, 'Tamami has not returned yet.'

'It shall remain locked tonight. It has been shut forever on Tamami. Tell him that when he comes,' Ustad Ramzi said, and retired to his room.

A few trainees were in the enclosure when this exchange took place and they spread the word. Those who had retired to their quarters also came out. Seeing them congregating in the akhara, Ustad Ramzi came out of his room and said: 'You have heard. The gate of the enclosure and the clay of the akhara is now closed to Tamami. If you see him, drive him away. These are your orders.'

The trainees were too shocked to say anything.

Ustad Ramzi's distrust of Tamami had been finally vindicated with all its horror. He did not think of reproving Tamami this time. He had struggled alone to guard his creed, he had tried to stem the disintegration of his world, but he had been failed again by the one on whom all his hopes were pinned. In the horrid new development of Tamami's addiction he saw the portents of a complete collapse of all that he cherished. It had not taken him long to come to his decision to excommunicate Tamami.

Tamami returned late at night and found the gate closed. As it always remained open, he pushed it to see if it had swung shut by itself. Realizing that it had been secured, he knocked. When nobody answered, he started banging on it. He called out the attendant's name. The attendant woke up when Tamami began rattling the gate violently. He watched Ustad Ramzi's window. There was no light in his room. Afraid of becoming a party to the brothers' feud, he quietly crept away into the darkness. Tamami was now calling out loudly and angrily for the gate to be opened. When no one responded, he fell quiet.

Ustad Ramzi heard Tamami shouting at the gate. He had not switched on the light in his room and was sitting on his bed in the darkness, still dressed. He did not move from his place.

Hearing Tamami shouting, a few neighbours came out of their houses. In the light from the municipal lamp they saw Tamami sitting on his haunches, leaning against the enclosure walls and Kabira talking to him. Someone had called him from his house. Tamami began to shake his head vehemently when Kabira repeatedly asked him to come with him. But Kabira did not give up and eventually Tamami accompanied him to his house.

———

The following day Ustad Ramzi rose before anyone had gotten up and long before the trainees started arriving in the akhara. He performed his routine tasks in the akhara with a lightness of body. When the first light of the morning appeared in the sky, Ustad Ramzi had his bath, said his prayers, filled the pitchers and went out to tend his rose bushes in the cemetery. He asked the enclosure attendant to send Tamami's belongings to Kabira's house. Then he retired to his room and did not come out for the rest of the day.

The next day was a Friday. In the afternoon there were few people in the akhara and it was quiet as usual.

Ustad Ramzi had not spoken a word after his directions were given to the attendant, but the events of the past days had become known and generated much gossip. When he came out of his room to leave for the Friday prayers, Ustad Ramzi noticed more than a few trainees gathered together in the enclosure. They became quiet as he approached.

Ustad Ramzi saw Tamami resting against the holy fig tree that stood near the gate. His legs were spread out and his back was turned towards the enclosure.

Anger welled up inside Ustad Ramzi at the sight of him. He snatched up a lathi standing by the gate, and stepped menacingly towards Tamami.

'Who let him in?' he shouted.

Tamami, who had not yet seen him, slowly turned his head. His face was drenched with tears. Ustad Ramzi felt strangely weakened by the sight, but grimly, he took possession of himself.

'Get out!' Ustad Ramzi roared. 'Get out!' he yelled once more and raised the lathi. At his words Tamami tried to move towards him and leaned on one of his arms to get up. Noticing that Tamami was still drugged Ustad Ramzi was filled with a blinding rage.

As Tamami came crawling towards him, he hit him with the lathi. But Tamami managed to cling to his legs. He sobbed loudly, mumbling something. Ustad Ramzi did not hear anything his brother said, nor was he any longer conscious of what he said himself. He wrenched himself away with all his force and brought the lathi down again across Tamami's back.

Kabira threw himself over Tamami.

'Enough, Ustad! Enough!' Kabira shouted.

Ustad Ramzi stopped.

'Get him out of here.' Ustad Ramzi gasped. 'I will not have this filth defile the clay of this akhara.'

'Ustad, he is your brother.'

'I don't wish to see his face again! Get him out this instant or I will kill him!'

Kabira rose, looking darkly at Ustad Ramzi, who was almost out of breath. Kabira tried to help the sobbing Tamami onto his feet. The enclosure attendant rushed out from his room to assist Kabira. A few trainees also stepped forward and accompanied Kabira and Tamami outside for a short distance until Kabira sent them back. When the trainees returned to the enclosure, Ustad Ramzi had already left for Friday prayers.

Later that day the enclosure attendant took Tamami's belongings to Kabira's house.

From that day Kabira stopped coming to Ustad Ramzi's akhara.

SINKING

At Kabira's house Tamami lapsed once again into addiction. Kabira told him he should fight for his right to live in the akhara. But for all his anger, Tamami did not question Ustad Ramzi's right as his elder, to turn him out of his own house. All he could think about was the manner in which he had been treated by his brother. Ustad Ramzi had neither accosted nor reprimanded him, but had just locked him out like some unclean creature without word or warning. When he had gone to ask for forgiveness, he had been beaten and chased away.

That the ties between them could be so easily severed – and that there would be no attempt at a rapprochement

by Ustad Ramzi – was something Tamami could neither understand nor bear. Only drugs brought him relief
from his pain.

INTERMEDIARY

Days passed. Then it was rumoured that Tamami was off drugs and Kabira had arranged for him to attend a makeshift akhara.

Gulab Deen was in a lively mood when he came to see Ustad Ramzi. He offered many apologies to Ustad Ramzi for not visiting earlier. He said it was not done out of disrespect, and enumerated many reasons for being held up.

'Tell me Ustad,' he finally asked, 'why is Tamami not exercising in this akhara? Forgive my saying this, but there are no differences between two brothers that cannot be resolved.' Without waiting for an answer, he added, 'Tell me that I can count on your forgiving him if I were to bring Tamami to you. A treasure is wasting before my eyes, Ustad! A treasure!'

Ustad Ramzi was infuriated by the promoter's suggestion that he exercised some influence over his own brother. In his heart he had not yet renounced his right to make decisions about Tamami's life.

'I wish to have nothing to do with him,' he replied. 'You can continue arranging fixed fights for him and making a living off it.'

'As God is my witness, Ustad, it was a true fight!' Gulab Deen swore, kissed his fingers with reverence, and raised them to touch his eyes. 'True as true! Sher Ali issued the challenge and Tamami accepted it. Fair as fair. I know of no fixing. Both men are hot-blooded and neither would agree to such a thing.'

Gulab Deen once again denied knowledge of any wrongdoing in the fight between Tamami and Sher Ali. Then he got up and took his leave of Ustad Ramzi.

━━━━

Everyone in Ustad Ramzi's clan reasoned that he may have turned Tamami out in a fit of anger, but that it would grieve him if they ostracized him as well, for in the end there would be a rapprochement between the brothers. Besides, they admired Tamami's talent and strength. When they learned that Tamami had started attending the makeshift akhara, they went there to assist him with his exercises and to spar with him.

Tamami had cut down on his exercises. He stopped after just a few hundred leg-squats. But the trainees were still unable to throw him off his feet. His robust constitution continued to triumph over the adverse effects of addiction even though he was still on drugs. Kabira often saw Gulab Deen take Tamami out in the evening. Since Tamami had no source of income, Kabira could guess where the drugs were coming from.

A couple of days later Tamami told Kabira that he had appointed him his manager.

'I have become your manager?' Kabira asked with some surprise.

'Yes, Kabira,' Tamami confessed in an embarrassed tone.

'And who appointed me? You?'

'Yes. Gulab Deen asked me to appoint you my manager so that someone could take care of my affairs.'

'Gulab Deen said that? Hunh!' Kabira's brow clouded over. There was something wrong with the way Gulab Deen was manipulating Tamami's professional affairs. It made Kabira apprehensive. He decided to have a word with Gulab Deen.

'Tamami will be fine once he sees that he does not need Ustad Ramzi to arrange his challenge fight,' Gulab

Deen told Kabira. 'He is still used to him making all his arrangements. You are his manager now. He trusts you and listens to you. Tell him that everything will be all right.'

When Kabira brought up Tamami's use of drugs, Gulab Deen looked at him in silence for a few moments. Then he spat out a shred of tobacco from his cigarette, and looked hard at Kabira with a strange gleam in his eyes.

'If Tamami loses a fight he could always win in a challenge bout.'

'Don't say that again!' Kabira cut in angrily. 'It is one thing for him to prolong an exhibition match. Throwing away a fight would destroy his name.'

'You are right,' Gulab Deen said in a changed tone. 'It will not do. We should ask Tamami to stop. He listens to you. First talk to him yourself, then, if you need me, I will come with you and we'll get our pahalwan to see the error of his ways.'

Gulab Deen's words had raised strange fears in Kabira's mind and he decided that he must go and see Ustad Ramzi to bring about a reconciliation between the brothers.

When Kabira mentioned his intention to Tamami, his face brightened.

Kabira was glad to see that.

———

A crisp wind was rustling the paling leaves on the branches of the banyan and holy fig trees. The sun was westering and its last light was falling on the gates of the akhara. Some trainees were arranging wooden planks outside the akhara and a few others were lying on wooden benches having their bodies rubbed with mustard oil.

Ustad Ramzi sat in his customary place by the side of the akhara. He shaded his eyes to see who it was that was entering the enclosure. The others had recognized Kabira and stopped their activities. It was Kabira's first visit since Ustad Ramzi had expelled Tamami from the akhara. The trainees regarded him inquisitively and when Kabira came up and greeted Ustad Ramzi, they drew nearer.

Ustad Ramzi had a feeling that everyone in the akhara was watching him. He felt his throat contract. He softly returned Kabira's greeting. Catching Ustad Ramzi's uneasy glance, one of the trainees brought a chair for Kabira. Another brought glasses of sardai.

Finally Kabira spoke: 'Ustad, Tamami made a mistake. I have come to ask you to forgive him.'

Ustad Ramzi was hardly looking at Kabira. He only heard the words. Now, more than ever, he felt the intense gaze of the trainees on him. He felt a sharp expectancy in them.

'When did he become such a lord that he could not come himself...'

'He will come. I will bring him, Ustad. He needs you,' Kabira said quickly and in one breath. 'Forgive him!'

'Forgive him for what?' Ustad Ramzi roared. 'For befouling the akhara with his deeds, this place which five generations had kept pure?'

As Kabira listened with his head bowed, Ustad Ramzi felt his resolve weakening. But he could feel the gaze of the trainees still riveted on him. It made him angry.

'Why does he need my forgiveness?' he sneered. 'He did not need me when he participated in the fixed bout and smeared his forefathers' honour. Now what does he need me for?

'He has a manager and a promoter now,' Ustad Ramzi's voice trembled as he cast a glance at Kabira. 'Souls find angels of their kind. Now all of you can win ever greater glories for yourselves.'

Ustad Ramzi's anger was spent. Kabira could have broken his defences with another plea, but he maintained a respectful silence.

The moment weighed heavily on Ustad Ramzi.

'Why don't you answer?' he shouted, more in irritation at the silence than to elicit a reply.

A few trainees moved forward to console Ustad Ramzi. They took charge of the situation and turned on Kabira:

'It would be best if you left now.'

'Ustad has not forgiven Tamami. Take him that message.'

'Why did he not come here himself ? Now he need not bother.'

Kabira quietly rose to his feet. Ustad Ramzi had turned his face away to master his feelings. Without speaking another word, Kabira left.

'Get lost! Don't show your face... I don't wish to see his face again!' Ustad Ramzi shouted after him.

———

Tamami was sitting up on his charpai carefully tying the folds of his turban. He had taken a bath and dressed, in expectation of his reconciliation with Ustad Ramzi. Hearing Kabira's footsteps he looked up, but the expression on Kabira's face immediately told him that his visit to Ustad Ramzi had been unsuccessful. Tamami's spirits sank.

He felt helpless again. His fixation on the title had made him dependent on Ustad Ramzi's acceptance of his life and actions. Even when he broke from him he did not break mentally from that relationship. Others, too, bound him to it. With Ustad Ramzi's overpowering hold on the affairs of the clan and the akhara, Tamami was always advised that his hopes lay in seeking Ustad Ramzi's forgiveness. The more Ustad Ramzi became distant, the more this possibility seemed remote to him. And when others saw how obsessed Tamami was with Ustad Ramzi's acceptance of him, the more they felt Tamami needed to address his relationship with Ustad Ramzi.

———

For the next few months Tamami fought several pahalwans in exhibition matches. Most of these bouts ended in draws. Using Tamami, Gulab Deen began to advance his small group of pahalwans of which Sher Ali was the most prominent. After his fight with Imama, which he had won on a technicality, Tamami was now considered a high-ranking pahalwan. When a pahalwan's bout with Tamami ended in a tie, his rank advanced. Gradually, pahalwans who did not have the same experience or skill as Tamami were held to be his equals. The clan elders saw what was happening, but were unable to do anything about it.

Soon, the crowds that came to see the fights grew impatient with Tamami's draws. They were the people who had watched Tamami train for his fight with Imama. They had rooted for him, applauding and jumping to their feet every time he performed a clever manoeuvre, but were disappointed at Tamami's winning so few of those bouts. When they saw that he did not use his advantages and gave the bouts away, they began heckling him. When even that did not bring about a change, they cheered Tamami's rivals.

Tamami's visits to the akhara became irregular. It was rumoured that he had had a falling out with Gulab Deen over the latter's promoting Sher Ali at Tamami's expense.

One day the news came that the police had arrested Tamami on charges of drug possession. The next day it was heard that he had been released after Gulab Deen posted bail for him. It was rumoured that the promoter had tipped off the police himself in order to place Tamami in his debt financially. Nobody knew the truth, but after that incident, Gulab Deen was seen exercising greater control over Tamami. He had also arranged a three-bout match between Tamami and Sher Ali.

———

Gulab Deen came to see Tamami at a time when he knew Kabira would not be around. Tamami greeted him nonchalantly. His body was beginning to show the impact of his addiction more visibly. He had lost weight. His girth had decreased and dark rings had appeared around his eyes. Tamami hadn't gone to the akhara again that day. He had been lying on the charpai since morning.

Gulab Deen said, 'Hope everything is going well with your routines,' as he looked around.

'Yes,' Tamami answered listlessly. 'Are the preparations for the bout done?'

'Preparations! Preparations! I don't know. To your question I would say both yes and no.'

Tamami looked up but did not ask what he meant. Since his arrest by the police – which Kabira had hinted was orchestrated by Gulab Deen – Tamami had developed a secret dread of the promoter.

'There are problems with the bout, Tamami,' Gulab Deen continued. 'I worry for you.'

A troubled look appeared on Tamami's face, but he remained silent. He was trying to concentrate his thoughts.

'This has to be a longer fight,' Gulab Deen said. 'You cannot finish it soon. And you must cede the first fight to Sher Ali.'

Tamami sat up. 'Kabira said I should not give away the fight,' he said angrily. 'I am not going to let Sher Ali defeat me! No!'

'Did I ask you to cede the series?'

'I am not going to lose the fight! Kabira told me you would ask me to lose a fight one of these days. I am not going to do it!' Tamami looked impatiently towards the door. He wished Kabira were there.

'Kabira is my friend too, and his advice is always good to have, especially since he is also your manager. But I have a very good reason for arranging the bout in this manner, Tamami. That reason I can only tell you, as it concerns you alone, not Kabira.'

'What reason?'

'It has to do with what happened between you and Ustad Ramzi.'

Tamami's expression remained tense, but he felt an anxiety mixed with eagerness.

'Brothers should not fight,' Gulab Deen continued. 'My heart has been heavy since Ustad Ramzi broke his ties with you. I could not do anything. But that does not mean you should be made to suffer. Enough is enough.'

Tamami now listened attentively.

'I went to see Ustad Ramzi the other day,' Gulab Deen said. 'I asked him to come and inaugurate the fight. But...' here Gulab Deen hesitated.

'But what?'

'He would not come. I said to him, Ustad Ramzi, do not bear ill will against your own brother. He would be honoured to have you at the akhara when he fights. He needs your blessings, I said.'

Tamami looked expectantly at the promoter.

'But Ustad Ramzi is a stern man – and proud. He suffers, but will not change his mind. Unless...'

'Unless what?'

'Unless he knows that the title would be lost by his clan if he did not come,' Gulab Deen said slowly. A few moments passed without Tamami commenting, but the promoter carried on confidently. 'You must lose the first fight. Then Ustad Ramzi will ask himself if it was because he was not there. He will see that his brother needs him. He is the way he is, but he would not willingly torment anyone. You know it as well as I do. What must be said to his credit, must be said. He is hurting too, and he will relent when he sees that you require him to be there with you. His pride will be satisfied and he will come for the second fight. The second fight could soon follow, perhaps in a month's time.'

'In a month's time...?'

'In a few weeks then,' Gulab Deen said quickly. 'Ustad Ramzi will come. And once he is there, he will find it hard not to reconcile with his brother. What happened between you is a shame, but blood is thicker than water. Now is our chance to correct the error. You decide. I have not told Kabira. He may not understand. If he speaks to someone in the clan, Ustad Ramzi might find out, and *then* he will never come. He is a proud man. You know your brother better than I do. You tell me if he would come if he were to find out.'

Tamami remained silent.

'Tell me if there is anything I can do,' Gulab Deen said.

'Are you sure Ustad Ramzi will come?' Tamami asked. 'How can you be certain?'

'Think carefully about what I have told you, then ask yourself. You will have the answer. Trust me, he will come.'

Tamami was quiet.

'There's another thing,' Tamami said as Gulab Deen prepared to leave.

'What?'

'I haven't had my…' Tamami began haltingly, 'I feel my head will break apart if I do not…'

———

The news spread quickly that Tamami had lost a fight to Sher Ali. It was also announced that the re-match would be held a month later. Kabira had accosted Tamami immediately after the bout, but Tamami refused to say anything.

'I feel exhausted,' he kept saying. 'You know I would not throw a fight.'

When he saw that Kabira did not believe him, Tamami began arguing and broke into tears. Kabira then went to see Gulab Deen, whom he had seen quietly slip away after the fight ended.

Kabira thought Tamami's body might be rebelling

against his drug addiction. Despite his vigil in the last weeks he had noticed that Tamami remained increasingly drugged. At times he would jump out of his charpai in the middle of the night, brushing his clothes wildly, complaining of insects crawling over his body. Kabira saw that there were no insects, either on Tamami's skin or on the charpai. Since summer, when he had kept the charpais in the sun, there had been no bedbugs either.

Sher Ali had looked strong in the akhara and was far more agile than Tamami. As Kabira was not certain that Tamami's defeat was entirely the result of Gulab Deen's orchestration, he was taken in by his convoluted arguments.

A rumour spread that Tamami had taken money from Sher Ali to draw the fight and that Tamami had done it to pay for his addiction. Kabira listened helplessly to the comments people made.

Kabira wondered if Ustad Ramzi would make up with Tamami, but he could not find the courage to broach the subject with him again.

———

Ustad Ramzi remained impassive upon hearing that Tamami had lost the bout to Sher Ali. It seemed that he had either expected the news, or else he was too sad to react in any way.

He wondered despondently if addiction and the lure of money had driven Tamami to lose fights and dishonour the prestige of his clan. Ustad Ramzi did not go to Gulab Deen to settle the matter with him, as some suggested. He told himself there was no point in doing so.

When a pahalwan held himself back before an opponent in an akhara, he betrayed his oath to the clay of the akhara. Tamami had broken his oath from greed. Once the faith with one's creed had been broken it did not stop at one disgrace; a storm of evils was bound to follow. In days to come there might be more. A canker was eating away at Tamami's soul and it could not be carved out to any perfection, Ustad Ramzi told himself.

With a final effort he shut his heart to Tamami and all thoughts of him.

ADDICT

Tamami's eyes looked sunken. His skin, which had once been radiant, looked pale. Weight loss had weakened his body. He complained of loss of appetite and did not consume even a third of the amount he ate when he had prepared to fight Imama. He complained that the food had no taste and stopped after eating a little. On occasion when he ate more at Kabira's insistence, he threw up soon afterwards. Frightened by what he saw, Kabira stopped insisting that he should increase his diet.

Kabira suggested Tamami see a hakim but Tamami refused to do so. When Kabira threatened to withdraw from his affairs if Tamami did not go see the hakim, Tamami said with bitterness, 'Everyone is forsaking me.

You and Ustad Ramzi and everyone else are all the same.'

Tamami's hands convulsed as he spoke, and the pitiable manner in which he complained made Kabira relent. When Kabira again pleaded that he visit a hakim, Tamami sullenly consented.

When the hakim pressed Tamami to disclose the quantity of drug he was using, he broke down and began yelling. Kabira had to take him away for fear of his becoming violent.

Tamami lay in a sombre mood at home. His respiration had become feeble. Kabira was worried that he would be sick again, but Tamami's condition gradually improved. He asked for water and drank an entire jug. That did not quench his thirst, and before half an hour had passed he complained again that his mouth was feeling parched. He drank another jug of water and fell asleep.

Kabira left the house on an errand and upon his return found Tamami sitting dressed on the charpai. He looked revived. Displaying complete presence of mind, he spoke about the second bout with Sher Ali.

Kabira decided to see Gulab Deen to ask for a change in scheduling.

The promoter was quite firm that the date of the fight could not be changed.

'Tamami would not want it,' Gulab Deen said, looking defiantly at Kabira.

'He cannot fight while he is in that condition,' Kabira protested.

'If he does not fight, it would mean that Sher Ali has won.'

'I will go and speak to Sher Ali.'

'Go! He will only tell you what you have already heard from me.'

As Gulab Deen had predicted, Kabira did not have any luck with Sher Ali. He was unwilling to change the date.

'Why are you asking for a postponement?' he asked. 'Is Tamami not well?'

'Tamami has just recovered,' Kabira swallowed his pride. 'I think he needs some more time to prepare.'

Sher Ali told him that he would be paid only if all the terms and conditions set by the promoter were met. If the fight were delayed by the pahalwans' consent, but without Gulab Deen's approval, their share of the proceeds from the ticket sales would be forfeited. Sher Ali said he could not afford that.

The amount received in Tamami's fee was too little to compensate Kabira for the money he had already spent on Tamami's training. Kabira had heard that Sher Ali had been paid a greater share of the proceeds of the tickets.

A week passed and Tamami got no worse, though at

the akhara his breaks between exercises grew longer with every passing day. The exercises had been curtailed, and he no longer ran laps. He could not grapple with more than two trainees at a time.

When they were alone one day, Kabira asked him if he wished to postpone the fight. Tamami suddenly turned upon him.

'Never! Never ever! I will fight! Nobody... not you nor anyone else will stop the fight!' He began to have trouble breathing and his hands shook. Kabira saw distrust in Tamami's eyes.

———

Tamami began to think that his punishment by Ustad Ramzi was justified. His anger at Ustad Ramzi's injustice surfaced briefly from time to time, but after a while it was buried under a sense of guilt which grew stronger when he saw that nobody except Kabira took his side.

He longed to exchange his situation with the one he had found unbearable before, and waited for the slightest hint of forgiveness from his brother that would have redeemed him in his own eyes. As his addiction grew worse, and impairment set into his nerves, all other thoughts were driven out of his mind with the exception of this one. Gradually it became a fixation.

———

One day when Kabira returned home, he found Tamami looking preoccupied. He asked Tamami if he wished to discuss anything with him.

'Ustad Ramzi will come to my fight, Kabira,' Tamami said in a soft and eager whisper.

Tamami had not mentioned Ustad Ramzi's name for several weeks.

'Let us hope he comes,' Kabira said.

'He will come,' Tamami said with an odd gleam in his eyes. 'I know that he will come.'

'Yes, hopefully he will come,' Kabira replied, unable to get Tamami's drift.

'You don't understand! He *will* come!' Tamami burst out. 'You don't want him to come! That's why you wanted to delay the fight! But the fight will not be delayed! He will come then!'

Feeling that Tamami needed to be reassured, Kabira replied, 'Yes Tamami, Ustad Ramzi will come. He will be there. I am sure of that.'

'Gulab Deen also said that,' Tamami said, as his expression changed to one of relief. 'So don't change anything. Don't ask Sher Ali to postpone the fight.'

Kabira wondered if Gulab Deen knew that Ustad Ramzi would come. He was not sure if there might not be some truth in that. Ustad Ramzi might relent; after all, he was Tamami's brother.

When Kabira ran into Gulab Deen, he asked him, 'Do you know if Ustad Ramzi is coming to the bout?'

'I don't know,' Gulab Deen quickly looked at him. 'Who told you he would come?'

'*You* told Tamami yourself!'

Gulab Deen smiled.

'Tamami asked me if he would come. I said he *may* come. I said I *think* he will come. That was all I told him. You know how he is these days. But I hope very much that Ustad Ramzi does come. A challenge fight lacks something without the blessing and presence of elders. Ustad Ramzi knows the venue where the bout is to be held. I will keep a chair for him in the front row. I will do all I can.'

'So, is he going to come or not?'

Gulab Deen did not answer his question but continued: 'I have heard rumours that he said he will come. But again, he may boycott the fight. These old ustads and their ways. Ustad Ramzi shouldn't think he is doing me a favour by coming. He should remember that it was I who arranged an exhibition match for Tamami when nobody was willing to fight him. There is no gratitude in my business. Everyone thinks I am after money. But what's wrong with that, you tell me? If I don't make money I go hungry. Do you know how hard I have worked to arrange this fight? Don't say you don't. But I get no thanks. Only complaints.'

Kabira could not tell how much of what the promoter said was true and how much of it was an act. Sometimes Kabira felt overwhelmed by Gulab Deen. He knew that if Tamami had an experienced manager he would have been treated with greater respect. But senior pahalwans kept their distance from Tamami for fear of crossing Ustad Ramzi.

FIXATION AND HOPE

On the morning of the fight Tamami's eyes shone brightly despite the dark rings around them. He was unable to hide his joy at the approach of the moment when he would see Ustad Ramzi in attendance at his fight. A smile played on his lips as he sat, with head bowed, while the barber cropped his hair. His anxiety grew as the hour of the bout neared, and when he left for the akhara he was on edge.

When they arrived at the akhara Kabira saw Gulab Deen getting his photographs taken with Sher Ali. Gulab Deen did not ask to have one taken with Tamami.

Tamami looked around and did not see Ustad Ramzi among those seated in the front row. Only three reserved chairs were left to be filled. One was occupied as he watched. Tamami recognized some members of his clan in the crowd, but noticing them avoid eye contact, he was filled with apprehension. He called Kabira over.

'Do you see Ustad Ramzi?' Tamami asked.

'No. But there is still time.'

'Others are here.'

'I saw them.'

'The fight won't begin until Ustad comes.'

'He will come. Just wait.'

Another seat was filled. A little before the fight, Tamami withdrew from the akhara and rushed towards the pavilion where the promoter was reviewing last-minute arrangements with a few other men. Kabira followed Tamami.

The trainees exchanged looks. It was against etiquette to withdraw from the akhara once the opponent had arrived.

'I am not going to fight without Ustad here,' Tamami shouted at Gulab Deen as he burst into the pavilion.

Gulab Deen signalled the other men to leave, and looked fixedly at Tamami.

'I won't fight without Ustad Ramzi,' Tamami repeated. His hands trembled.

'The fight starts in ten minutes,' Gulab Deen said coolly. 'It will be held on time.'

'But he is not here.'

'Who is not here?'

'Ustad Ramzi.'

Gulab Deen snapped up some dried fruits from the top of his desk. 'Whether he is here or not, the fight will be held. I cannot pamper you like a baby. If you are not in the akhara when the dhol is beaten to open the fight, Sher Ali will be declared the winner.'

'We can wait a little longer for Ustad Ramzi.' Kabira spoke up. 'Maybe he will come.'

'A few minutes, not indefinitely,' Gulab Deen replied. 'There are people outside who have bought tickets. They are here to watch a fight, and a fight they will see, whether...'

'I could send someone to see if he is coming...' Kabira quickly said.

'Don't say *if* and *maybe!* You told me Ustad Ramzi would come,' Tamami turned on Kabira. Then he faced Gulab Deen again, saying, 'You said he was coming. Where is he?'

'Listen to me Tamami!' Gulab Deen said sharply. 'Listen to me carefully, now!'

Tamami fell silent. He looked angry, but confused.

'You want Ustad Ramzi to be here so that he sees you fight. But Ustad Ramzi is a proud man. And you know he loves you. Don't deny it. I know well that you know it. Good! Now I am not saying that this will happen, but it is a possibility. He may say to himself: "Tamami did things I did not like. Therefore I excommunicated him. I want to see what he can do when he is left on his own." This is what he tells himself. Now let me tell you what happened next. Tamami went away, and before anybody knew it, he got himself a manager, and also a promoter. Now Kabira is your good friend and I am here to serve you: it's my job, and no credit to me. But now Ustad Ramzi is surprised and also happy and not a little proud. Tamami is no longer a small boy. A challenge match comes next. Ustad Ramzi is carefully watching to see what Tamami will do. And what does Tamami do? He throws the bout. Why? Because Tamami can easily afford to do it. Why? Because Tamami is far stronger than Sher Ali. But the results create suspense. Ustad Ramzi does not say a word, but I know how he feels in his heart. He says to himself: "Maybe Tamami has fallen before Sher Ali's might." I will tell you why he thinks that. Sher Ali is not a *nobody*. That was why he was matched with Tamami. Ustad Ramzi may say what he likes, but in his heart he knows Sher Ali is no ordinary pahalwan. So he says to himself: "What would happen if I went there and Tamami again drew the bout, or, God forbid, lost it? Would I be able to show my face to the world? While the Ustad-e-Zaman looked on, his brother was defeated by a relatively unknown pahalwan. No! No! No! A hundred times *no!*" But as you see, Ustad Ramzi does not know that Tamami also has a plan.'

Gulab Deen winked mischievously at Kabira and Tamami before continuing: 'Ustad Ramzi does not know that Tamami is playing a cat-and-mouse game with Sher Ali. Of course, Ustad Ramzi has no way of knowing it. He is confused. Only one thing will help him see things as they *really* are.' The promoter got up and grasping Tamami and Kabira by their forearms walked them to the entrance of the pavilion. 'And that thing is to fight and defeat Sher Ali. Tamami will make the contest even by winning this bout, and in the next one Tamami will rout Sher Ali.'

Gulab Deen then looked around and said in a conspiratorial manner: 'I should be careful with my words. If one of Sher Ali's supporters heard me, I would be in big trouble. They would think I was conspiring against their pahalwan with Tamami and his manager. Now we are not doing that, are we? Ha! Ha! Ha! Ha!'

'He is not here,' Tamami looked at the only empty seat that was visible from the pavilion. Devoid of anger, his words sounded more like a complaint.

'I told you. Ustad Ramzi will not be here. But he will be waiting. Waiting for the news of Tamami making him proud, and to receive the victory procession. Everything will be forgotten then. But to the akhara now – we don't want to keep Ustad Ramzi waiting.'

Tamami's voice choked up as he spoke. He did not seem to address anyone in particular: 'I will go back to the akhara if I win. I will ask his forgiveness. He will forgive me.'

'Yes, Tamami,' Gulab Deen said, casting a sharp glance at Kabira. 'But you must hurry. The sooner you finish the fight the sooner you can go before Ustad Ramzi. The sooner you will be reunited.'

'Then I will fight!' Tamami said resolutely, wiping away a tear.

'Yes! Yes! Tamami will fight! Tamami will prove himself to Ustad Ramzi once and for all!' the promoter said, looking at Kabira.

Kabira did not wish to argue with the promoter with Tamami in that state of mind. He felt totally helpless against Gulab Deen's tricks. He cursed him in his heart, but remained quiet.

'Kabira, I want you to be my witness,' Tamami said. 'Be my witness that I fulfilled my promise to Ustad Ramzi.'

'Yes Tamami, I will,' Kabira said.

His heart was heavy as he led Tamami to the akhara. He was no longer able to think clearly. He was afraid now. A vague fear took hold of him as the beat of the dhol rose to a crescendo.

There had been a lot of rumours about Tamami's health and addiction. Some debased sense of excitement in the cruel spectacle had drawn a larger crowd than the earlier bout.

When Tamami removed the coverlet from his body, the audience saw that his body had shrunk. His muscles had become slack, and the tendons were clearly visible under the skin as in an old man's body. While the drugs had done their damage to Tamami's body, they had been unable to completely wreck the mass of muscle and bone. Tamami still towered over the quiet, grim-looking Sher Ali.

'Even a dead elephant is worth a lakh-and-a-quarter,' someone from the spectators commented.

Sher Ali did a few leg-squats in his corner, then took off his robe and faced Tamami defiantly. A month of preparation had made a difference to his constitution as well. He looked better prepared than he had the last time.

Tamami cast a last look at the last empty chair and went to his corner in the akhara. A few in the crowd hooted at him, but he did not pay attention.

At the referee's signal, Sher Ali cut a circle around Tamami and locked him in a triceps and triceps tie-up.

Then he ducked, and sweeping under Tamami's arm, he emerged at his back, led Tamami into a breakdown, and reached for an inside crotch hold.

The crowd applauded and cheered him.

'Ride him! Ride him now!' they shouted.

'Soon! Soon!' Tamami shouted back, imagining the crowd cheered for him.

People broke into laughter at his retort.

Kabira felt as if someone had stabbed him through the heart.

'Ride, Sher Ali! Ride him!' someone shouted, and Tamami raised his head. The look of shock in his eyes turned the next moment into a scowl.

Sher Ali tried to climb onto his leg. As Tamami rose, Sher Ali inserted his leg between Tamami's. He pushed Sher Ali's knee, making it impossible for him to move back on top to maintain his crossbody ride. Sher Ali slid off Tamami's shoulder. Tamami quickly tried to rise to his feet, but for a moment everything went dark before his eyes. He reeled. Sher Ali, already on his knees, lurched forward to tackle Tamami's legs. Tamami threw his weight forward even as he was pushed back. He landed on his hips on the akhara clay, facing the empty chair in the first row.

Tamami weighed more than Sher Ali and while Sher Ali's manoeuvre was foiled, he had already moved too far down across his adversary's body for Tamami to gain any advantage. Suddenly Sher Ali saw Tamami rise and reach out.

'He's here. He's come,' Tamami mumbled.

Without thinking of a possible motive for Tamami's strange behaviour, Sher Ali took advantage of this shift of balance to gain his feet, and immediately threw his weight backwards, pulling Tamami down with him. Tamami, who failed to apply the counter, fell awkwardly. His neck bent under the joint weight of his and Sher Ali's bodies. To avert the building pressure on his neck he turned using all his strength, and both his shoulders briefly touched the ground.

Sher Ali disengaged and jumped to his feet when the dhol began beating. He bolted to his corner to do a victory dance.

Tamami's face looked drained. There was no sign of Ustad Ramzi. The chair was empty.

The uproar of the audience even drowned the beat of the dhol.

———

The spectators had thinned out. Kabira and Tamami were the only ones left with the promoter in his pavilion. Tamami had been drinking water constantly and still felt thirsty. Kabira angrily pushed away the jug of water.

'Tell him he can challenge Sher Ali,' he addressed Gulab Deen sharply.

'Of course he can challenge him. Everyone knows that.'

'When? Arrange it for this week. We will declare it this very day. I will go and talk to Sher Ali.'

'You are forgetting something.'

'What?'

'Tamami cannot fix the date.'

'Why not?'

'The winner decides that. He decides when the challenge fight will be held.'

Kabira was struck silent. He now understood the reason for the promoter's defiant tone and his testiness, and he felt a sudden rage.

'You are responsible for all this!'

'Responsible for what?' Gulab Deen started gathering the receipt books on his desk.

'How early can the challenge fight be held?' Kabira asked after a moment.

'In a few months, maybe. Maybe more. It all depends. Sher Ali might wish to postpone it further. You know he wants to fight some exhibition matches – make some money. That's what I think he will do. But I have to go now. Come see me when you think he is ready.'

Kabira felt a hint of derogation in the way the promoter pointed towards Tamami.

'Come over next week and we will settle our account,' Gulab Deen told him as he stepped out.

———

Tamami had only half-listened to the conversation between Kabira and Gulab Deen.

'Ustad Ramzi did not come,' he said as Kabira led him back home.

Kabira did not reply.

'He did not come, Kabira,' Tamami's voice broke. 'He will not come now. He will never forgive me.'

Kabira still remained silent.

Tamami was occupied with only one thought: any possibility of a rapprochement with Ustad Ramzi was now forever lost. He began to cry.

After escorting him home Kabira brought some food for him. Before leaving the room he asked Tamami to get some rest and sleep for a few hours.

Tamami could not sleep. Every time he closed his eyes he felt his predicament more acutely. He tried to ward off that oppressive weight. But a swirling darkness surrounded him. He felt more depressed than ever. His hands desperately searched his dirty clothes and discovered a small packet carefully tied with a rubber band.

———

Kabira had kept a strict watch on Tamami, but it had slipped Kabira's mind to search the dirty laundry. When he returned home he found Tamami lying face down on the floor, the viscous fluid from his nose slowly pooling around his head.

He had been dead from a drug overdose for several hours.

SANCTITY

After the post-mortem Kabira collected the body from the morgue.

Ustad Ramzi lay awake on the charpai later that night when the enclosure attendant entered his room.

'Ustad...' the attendant said.

Without getting up, Ustad Ramzi turned towards him, but the attendant remained silent.

'What is it?'

'They have come.'

'Who has come?' Ustad Ramzi asked, looking blankly at him.

'They are asking for you.'

Ustad Ramzi got up and stepped out of the room.

Nobody had turned on the enclosure lights, but Ustad Ramzi could make out the figures sitting around a bier draped with white sheets. There was a smell of camphor in the air. He stopped at a distance.

'What do you want?' he called out.

One among them got up and stepped towards him. It was Kabira.

'We have brought Tamami's body here,' Kabira said.

'Why did you bring him here?' Ustad Ramzi asked.

'We have brought him here to be buried, Ustad.'

'You brought him here to be buried? But these gates have been closed on him.'

Kabira seemed to struggle with himself for a moment. His voice trembled when he spoke: 'The time for disputes and forgiveness is now past, Ustad, Tamami is dead.'

A few more people got up from around Tamami's bier and came forward. Ustad Ramzi recognized Maulvi Yameen and one of Tamami's friends from the neighbourhood.

'Take him back!' Ustad Ramzi suddenly raised his voice. 'He was expelled for desecrating the place! These grounds are hallowed! He cannot be buried here! Take him away! Take him…!'

More people entered the akhara. These were members of Ustad Ramzi's clan who had arrived when they heard that Tamami's bier had been brought to the enclosure. As they gathered behind Ustad Ramzi, he turned towards them.

'The burial cannot be allowed here! Those who have broken the creed cannot be buried in these grounds.' Ustad Ramzi's voice was composed.

The members of his clan looked at him.

'Death removes all differences, Ustad,' Kabira spoke again.

'Ask them to leave. It is not warranted, tell them.' Ustad Ramzi repeated, looking at the members of his clan.

They stared back, unsure of what he meant.

'Maulvi Yameen!' Kabira called out. 'Explain to him...! He will listen to you.'

'Ustad Ramzi...' Maulvi Yameen began.

'Take him away! Take him away! Tell them to take him away!' Ustad Ramzi shouted, turning towards Maulvi Yameen.

Maulvi Yameen said to Kabira, 'Do not let this argument delay the burial.'

'Even animals respect death,' Kabira hissed. 'Even animals know better.'

'All places are equal,' Maulvi Yameen said. 'We can bury him in the municipal graveyard.'

'Yes. Bring him away.' Kabira wiped his eyes. 'Bring

him away, as God sees all. He will not respect the honour due to the dead,' he said pointing at Ustad Ramzi, 'but we must not disgrace it. Pick him up. Pick him up now! We are leaving!'

Driven by the authority in Kabira's voice the men in Kabira's group stepped forward to lift Tamami's bier.

Ustad Ramzi watched Kabira and his friends carry it away. All the members of his clan and the trainees who had come out from their quarters followed them. The enclosure grew darker as the men left, reciting prayers for the dead.

When the enclosure attendant, who was the last to leave to join the funeral procession, turned back to close the gate behind him he saw Ustad Ramzi standing rigid and unmoved in his place.

For Ustad Ramzi it was not just Tamami's life that had ended with his death. Tamami's slide into degeneration that would have brought further disgrace and ruin to his clan was finally over. So was Ustad Ramzi's own exhausting journey through the pits of humiliation and shame.

RECKONING

When Ustad Ramzi had excommunicated Tamami using his authority as the head of the clan, everyone followed his orders. The clan members felt that Tamami's punishment was disproportionate to his actions, yet their own interests were tied to the clan. Ustad Ramzi's actions gave them a sense of moral superiority that allowed them to feel outraged at his deed while maintaining an attitude of just indignation towards Tamami.

The side of human nature that takes delight in the spectacle of others' misery had revealed itself in the comments the clan members and trainees made in passing even before Tamami's death:

'It was too harsh of him to expel his own brother from the enclosure.'

'But Tamami had crossed all limits.'

'Still, he was his brother. Born of the same mother.'

'But Tamami had rolled his name and his family honour into the dust.'

After Tamami's death Ustad Ramzi had vowed to carry on as if nothing had changed. But when he stepped out of his quarters he felt hostile eyes following his movements.

The one who was dead had escaped condemnation. But the other was alive and was judged:

'Ustad Ramzi was heartless to deny the clan burial grounds to his own brother.'

'He first expelled his brother from his home and then denied him even a burial with his forefathers.'

'Why should he expect those who are not his kin to show him any mercy?'

Ustad Ramzi heard these remarks and kept quiet. But now he had recurring dreams in which he saw his brother's dead body lying without a winding sheet at his feet.

REPROACH

When Ustad Ramzi stepped out of the enclosure on the fourth day after Tamami's death to visit Gohar Jan's kotha, he felt nauseous. He kept wandering off the path and walked aimlessly in the adjoining alleys.

He had summoned all his fortitude to drive the thoughts of his brother out of his mind. But he did not succeed in quelling his conscience from which fragments of guilt broke out. An unresolved conflict now festered in his mind. He had tried to subdue the commotion in his soul and failed.

When he was the foremost pahalwan of his day, he had defended his elders' titles until they retired. But it was also true that he never had any dearth of worthy competitors. Those were the times that produced great ustads and champions. A month never went by without a major bout or tourney. He had always had the incentive to remain in a state of constant physical preparedness and his gruelling routine never tired him mentally.

But nobody came forward to fight Tamami after Imama's death. There was no challenger in sight, but Tamami underwent a punishing regime of exercises day after day, week after week. If Ustad Ramzi had retired at that time, the Ustad-e-Zaman's title would have brought some consolation to Tamami who would have found in it an acknowledgement of his struggle. But he could not bring himself to accept that Tamami was worthy of a title that he had held.

He had turned his brother into his personal slave, fighting the shadows of his own fears. His actions did not serve the art he professed to protect; they served only him. Tamami's inability to protest his treatment must have driven him to despair.

Ustad Ramzi found himself not far from Gohar Jan's kotha entrance. He craved some reprieve from his suffocating grief, and the darkness of the unlighted stairwell offered itself as a refuge to him.

Ustad Ramzi climbed up the stairwell and sat down midway.

He was sure Gohar Jan would have learned of Tam-ami's death. Everyone in the inner city knew about it. Banday Ali, who usually came to inquire if he was absent without notice, had not visited him for three days. Ustad Ramzi's presence at the kotha would oblige Gohar Jan to adhere to the usual routine of her recitals. He was not sure if he desired that.

Ustad Ramzi regretted having come there, and felt he would be sick.

As he rose to leave, he heard someone coming up the stairs.

'The bulb is fused again! What a nuisance!' he heard Banday Ali say.

'Who's there?' Banday Ali asked hearing Ustad Ramzi's footsteps on the staircase.

'It's me!' Ustad Ramzi called out.

'I am coming up,' Banday Ali said.

He passed Ustad Ramzi on the way up and opened the door. The bulb in the veranda lit up part of the stair-case too, but Ustad Ramzi did not move into the light. Banday Ali stepped over to one side.

'Come on inside. I will go and change the bulb,' he said.

Ustad Ramzi stepped inside.

Entering the Music Room, he found Gohar Jan by herself. The tanpura and the tablas were covered.

'Please sit down,' Gohar Jan said, motioning him to his regular place on the carpet.

Ustad Ramzi sat silently.

He felt cold. It was not yet September, but in the evenings the air had become crisp and dry. He felt thirsty.

'Can I have some water?' he asked.

Gohar Jan poured him some water from the ewer.

'I heard of your brother's death,' she said, passing the bowl. 'I am sorry.'

Ustad Ramzi gripped the bowl with both hands. But he saw she was not looking at him.

'I heard that you two were the only members of your family. One never forgets a childhood spent together.'

He stared at her. His pride and guilt put him on guard at her first words, but now his concentration wavered. Because of their significant age difference, he and Tamami had had no shared childhood. It was also said about Ustad Ramzi that childhood never visited him. He had always been serious and sombre.

'Sometimes it is a difficult thing,' Gohar Jan's voice interrupted Ustad Ramzi's thoughts, 'to go through life carrying all the memories of your family, knowing that both the memories and family will end with you.'

Gohar Jan said something a moment later which Ustad Ramzi did not quite hear, but it registered sufficiently on his mind to attract his attention.

'... I could talk about it,' she said, 'as I do not have many years left.'

Something more than the words caught Ustad Ramzi's ear. It was the grief in Gohar Jan's voice, so much at odds with her usual tone.

Then Ustad Ramzi's attention wandered away. He could not tell how long his mind was blank. When he regained his attention, Gohar Jan was saying: 'A girl's face is the only memory I have of our family. She may have been my sister, younger than myself, for I remember her following me around the house. I don't know if my father was around, but I can feel the presence of my mother. It surprises me sometimes that I do not recall her features. My sister's face is all I remember. I wonder if she remembers me still. It is a harsh sentence to know that somewhere, someone who was a part of you and whom you will never see, perhaps still lives. The thought has not left me since the day I was separated from my family.'

Gohar Jan fell silent. It was the first time that she had mentioned her family.

An incident of many years ago rose with great vividness from some vault of Ustad Ramzi's memory at her words.

When Tamami was eight or nine, he had stolen some guavas from a neighbour's tree. The neighbour had complained to the elders. Fearful of the punishment that lay in store for him, Tamami had come running to his brother. He was still carrying the guavas in the folds of his kurta, and his mouth was full of the half-unripe fruit as he mumbled, 'Don't tell anyone!' and slid under the charpai where Ustad Ramzi was sitting. Shortly afterwards one of the ustads had entered the enclosure with a rattan cane in his hand. He looked around and asked, 'Have you seen Tamami?' Ustad Ramzi stood up, exposing Tamami who was still nibbling at the guava. He was pulled out by his ear and dragged away. Tamami had cried and tried to clutch on to his legs, but he did not intervene.

As he recalled that scene now, Ustad Ramzi realized he could have saved Tamami a beating that day.

Ustad Ramzi felt a constriction in his chest. He could think of nothing but Tamami. His heart was pulsing and beating with the usual rhythm, but with a strength that was almost painful. All his senses were alert but he felt that his heart was sinking.

'Are you all right?' Gohar Jan asked.

'I do not feel well, I'm sorry,' he said with his eyes lowered.

Gohar Jan offered him another bowl of water.

'I think I must go,' he said returning the empty bowl.

'Rest your mind,' she said to him as he got up.

The door had been left open and he quietly walked out.

By the time he reached the enclosure his nauseous feeling had subsided.

———

That night Ustad Ramzi again dreamt of Tamami.

He dreamt he was alone in the enclosure. The sand swept past him in waves. Something came floating over it from his right, and a smell like camphor's – only stronger and strangely altered, and so strong he could almost taste it – assailed his senses. The object came to rest at his feet. It was a human body clad in winding sheets. Without seeing the covered face, he knew it was Tamami's corpse. He tried to step away but could not. He tried to reach down to touch the sand but felt dizzy. Then a crow alighted at his feet and began digging into the sand with its beak. He stepped back in terror. The smell was still in his nostrils when his eyes opened. He sat up and stepped out into the courtyard where the freshly smoothed clay of the akhara shone in the moonlight.

He could no longer avoid answering the questions which had haunted him since Imama's death, and had subsequently taken on new meaning.

Did the essence of his art not lie in creating a delicate harmony between strength and the opposing force? Did it not lie in keeping power bridled?

When he had set out Tamami's training routine these had not been his considerations. It had caused the death of two men. He had then aggravated his crime by a false sense of rectitude.

The base passions that he had detected in Tamami lived inside himself: in his anger, ambition, and pride.

In obedience to them he had compromised every principle he sought to save and disgraced himself more than words could express.

The guilt Ustad Ramzi carried in his heart etched his face in this moment of reckoning.

———

He visited Tamami's grave. There were no other graves beside it. Marked with a tombstone commemorating Tamami's life, it was surrounded by budding rose bushes planted by Kabira. After saying the benediction Ustad Ramzi sat down at the foot of the grave where the caretaker found him when he made his rounds at night.

RETIREMENT

The clan wondered what motivated Ustad Ramzi to remove his fighter's belt and retire. It did seem to them that Ustad Ramzi had aged many years in one day. He had turned old and haggard overnight.

The trainees kept the akhara in use, turning and smoothing the clay on alternate days. A few older pahalwans still came to the akhara, more out of habit than anything else. Sometimes when an exhibition bout was held, the place came to life. The senior pahalwans supervised the contestants' training regime, and judged their fights. Then quiet returned to the place.

Lost in his thoughts, Ustad Ramzi kept a silent watch on everything from his seat by the side of the akhara.

He did not react to promoter Gulab Deen advancing his coterie of pahalwans through rigged bouts. He similarly remained impassive when the promoter instituted new titles and some members from Ustad Ramzi's clan broke away and joined the promoter's group.

Ustad Ramzi continued his visits to Gohar Jan's kotha. Sometimes she noticed him sitting with a vacant air, often staying longer than usual as if he had lost his sense of time.

A few times the trainees heard Ustad Ramzi crying in the cemetery.

CHANGES

Ustad Ramzi's enclosure was re-zoned into the commercial district. Subsequently, it attracted the interest of builders. Aware of the news that the imposition of a higher property tax had added to Ustad Ramzi's financial troubles, the builders' representatives had approached him and offered a substantial contribution to the clan if he would agree to sell the land. They did not hide the fact that they planned to build on the site. They explained that the graves in the cemetery would be moved to the municipal graveyard at their cost and in accordance with the religious law.

Ustad Ramzi turned them down.

Gohar Jan's enclave was re-zoned as well. She was disturbed to hear of plans by the municipality to declare buildings in the tawaifs' enclave as hazardous for living and have them demolished. With necessary repairs the buildings could have had a long life, but none of the tawaifs, including Gohar Jan, had the money for the extensive renovations needed. The builders had already made offers for properties in the enclave.

Gohar Jan knew that the age and condition of the buildings were not the only factors behind the municipal councillors' decision. The builders' money was behind it. Their plans were abetted by recent objections raised about the tawaifs' enclave. A new wave of immigrants whose attempts to squat in the enclave had been unsuccessful objected to the tawaifs' kothas on moral grounds. That propaganda had made it easier for the municipal authorities to act.

———

The monsoon had returned and it was raining heavily. One afternoon when there was a lull, Banday Ali found two men in khaki uniforms standing in the alley scribbling in their logbooks. A while later they started knocking on the doors of the kothas.

'What is it about?' Banday Ali asked when they knocked on the door.

'Municipal inspection,' one of the men said. The supervising inspector looked sullenly at Banday Ali.

'What is it for?' Banday Ali said.

'You will find out soon enough,' he replied, stepping in. 'How many rooms do you have here?'

The supervisor also entered and began to look around. Then he saw the signs of water seepage on the ceiling.

'Make a note of this,' he said to his subordinate. 'Very risky.'

Gohar Jan entered the room and stopped when she found Banday Ali with strangers. 'Who're these people?'

'Municipal inspectors,' Banday Ali answered.

'We need to see the other rooms,' the supervisor said.

'Come this way, please,' Banday Ali conducted them inside after Gohar Jan nodded her permission.

The ceiling of the Music Room was also leaking. The municipal inspectors noted the bucket that had been placed under the leak to collect the rainwater.

'The place is falling apart,' the supervisor said. 'How long ago was it constructed?'

'It was built ninety-five years ago,' Gohar Jan answered. 'The construction is sturdy. Only the ceiling needs some repairs.'

The supervisor sniggered but said nothing.

'What is the purpose of this inspection?' Banday Ali asked.

'To determine whether or not the building is habitable.'

'It is habitable. It just needs repairs,' Gohar Jan said calmly.

'Please listen,' Banday Ali said to the supervisor. 'Sometimes there are small cracks like these in new constructions, too. Once the rains are over, we will get the repairs done. All the roof needs is a new layer of plaster. That is all. The building itself is very sturdy.'

'Do whatever you like,' the supervisor said looking around. The other man noted something in his logbook.

'At least make a note that the roofs will be plastered in a month's time,' Banday Ali insisted.

The subordinate looked at the supervisor.

'Yes, yes. We have noted it down,' the supervisor said, casting an angry glance at his subordinate.

'When will we know the results of your inspection?' Gohar Jan asked.

'The municipality will send you a letter.'

'Do you know when?'

'We don't know all that. Once the inspection is done you will hear from the municipal office,' he replied as he turned towards his companion. 'Let's go.'

Banday Ali saw them look around as they went out.

'Ask the old man now,' Banday Ali heard the supervisor whisper as he saw them out.

'What time is the mehfil tonight?' the subordinate asked.

'There are no mehfils here now,' Banday Ali replied.

The supervisor stepped out of the door, but the other lingered.

'Don't lie,' he said. 'I saw the ankle-band and the instruments.'

'What is he saying?' the superior shouted from the bottom of the stairwell.

'We will pay,' the man said patting the wallet in his breast-pocket.

'No mehfils are held here,' Banday Ali said curtly and began closing the door on him. 'This is a private residence now.'

A scowl appeared on the man's face but Banday Ali had shut the door.

When he came inside he saw that Gohar Jan looked pensive.

'I do not have a good feeling about it,' Banday Ali said. 'You should go straight to the mayor. You know him... He will not refuse you.'

'He may, or may not.'

'But we may not have a roof over our heads soon...'

'There's still time. Let me think carefully about it.'

———

In the continuing daily rains Ustad Ramzi's enclosure was inundated by the overflow from the sewers of the inner city. Sewage water stood waist-high over the graves of Ustad Ramzi's forefathers in the cemetery. He had to herd the peacocks into a shed in the enclosure, but it was a small place, and he felt sorry when dirt soiled their tail feathers.

It was alleged by many that the builders had conspired to divert the sewer water to Ustad Ramzi's enclosure. The walls of the drains had been breached overnight. But no one was caught or seen making the breach. Ustad Ramzi had no proof.

The rains became less intense, but did not end. It was a near impossibility to drain such a large area with manual help because the sloping land had made it a natural pool.

Having failed in their attempts to drain the water by carrying it away in buckets, the trainees told Ustad Ramzi that it would be futile to continue with the labour until the rains stopped. Ustad Ramzi, who had worked with them, realized that this request was not motivated by a lack of will. It was simply not practical to go on. And yet the sight of the graveyard inundated with sewage did not let him have any peace.

One morning Ustad Ramzi put on all his decorations and medals and tied a starched turban on his head in preparation for a visit to the municipal director.

After a long wait the clerk called out his name. He parted the dusty curtains and entered the office whose sole occupant was a shrivelled, bespectacled man. Without looking up, he wrote steadily in a file which lay open before him. Ustad Ramzi softly mumbled a greeting. Receiving no response, he hesitantly drew out one of the empty chairs, and sat down to wait for the director to finish his work.

A few moments later the director raised his head and looked at Ustad Ramzi. Thinking that perhaps the director had forgotten his name, Ustad Ramzi introduced himself and briefly told him about his renowned clan's history.

The director listened to Ustad Ramzi's recital impassively and without interruption. Ustad Ramzi finally explained the situation and requested that the director send over one of the trucks fitted with pumping equipment to his enclosure. He offered to pay the expense of the staff required to do the work.

The director listened to his request with a growing expression of incredulity and then replied in a studied tone of voice, 'It is not possible to send government equipment on private business. Once that sort of thing starts it will throw the functioning of the department into disarray. I have disciplined the staff on previous occasions for such activities. Where would I stand if I were to sanction such a thing myself?'

Ustad Ramzi spoke a little excitedly then, reminding him that the akhara was taxed as a commercial property, and it was the responsibility of the municipality to provide assistance when required.

The municipal director sat back in his chair, clasped his hands together as if to compose his thoughts, and after a few moments of silence began to explain impassively that his resources were already constrained. He could not keep offering favours. He did not mean any disrespect to the dead, but the living had a greater right to municipal services. And it was best for the dead to sleep in graveyards. He had heard recently that the builders had made Ustad Ramzi an offer to that effect. He wondered why Ustad Ramzi did not move the graves to the graveyard and the akhara elsewhere.

There had been complaints about stagnant water from other parts of the inner city as well, he told Ustad Ramzi, and if a recommendation was made, and one or more tankers were assigned to drain the areas, Ustad Ramzi's request would be considered on its merit. He could fill out a complaint form on the way out.

Ustad Ramzi quietly took his leave and stepped outside. His hands shook as he filled out the complaint form. During the humiliating interview he had controlled his anger more than once.

When he visited Gohar Jan's place that evening it was drizzling again. The Music Room's roof was still leaking. At regular intervals a few drops fell into the vessel on the floor.

After the recital ended Gohar Jan looked searchingly at Ustad Ramzi.

He had not touched the cup of tea that had been offered to him. Hearing a crack of thunder Ustad Ramzi started and made to leave, but Gohar Jan stopped him.

'You look preoccupied. What is the matter?'

Ustad Ramzi mentioned the flooding in the graveyard and his visit to the municipality. He told her he had decided to go and plead again with the director.

'Your rose garden must have been damaged too,' Gohar Jan said after a moment's silence.

Ustad Ramzi remained quiet.

'You must not worry,' Gohar Jan said as Ustad Ramzi was leaving. 'It is a matter of a cemetery's sanctity. The municipality will act on your request, I am sure.'

Her words did not console Ustad Ramzi.

'Please remember to send Ustad Ramzi some of your red rose branches,' Gohar Jan said to Banday Ali, who had come to remove the teacup.

'Certainly.'

'Banday Ali says he has cultivated this variety himself,' Gohar Jan said, turning towards Ustad Ramzi with a smile. 'He claims it does not grow wild as often, when manured with used Darjeeling tea leaves.'

'That I guarantee,' Banday Ali smiled. 'And once the stocks have taken root, I shall·keep you supplied with scions.'

———

Two days after Ustad Ramzi's visit to the municipality offices no action had been taken by the authorities. To complicate matters, it rained heavily again one night. In the two intervening days he had filled buckets in the graveyard's pool and carried and emptied them into the main sewer, no longer caring if and when the rains would stop.

The water level had receded a few inches as a result of the trainees' and Ustad Ramzi's efforts, but his knees had been hurting so badly that by the middle of the next day he was bedridden and unable to put his weight on his feet any longer. The hakim had been called and he prescribed Ustad Ramzi medicine for the inflammation of the joints.

He woke up the next morning early as usual, but lay in bed, marshalling all his energy against the lingering exhaustion that was compounded by a sense of helplessness. The medicine offered little help. The skies were again overcast, and the sandpipers and rain crows circled overhead, clamouring for more rains.

Ustad Ramzi was still in bed around ten o'clock when he heard loud voices in the enclosure, and the noise of some heavy vehicle driving in. Limping out of his room, he saw the municipality truck parking along the cemetery walls. He forgot all about his pain and for a few minutes stood watching dumbfounded.

'It was the matter of a cemetery's sanctity,' he muttered to himself.

The contingent of municipal workers quickly got down to work. Later in the afternoon, a supervisor also dropped in to see how the work was progressing. In two days the cemetery was completely drained. It had showered a little during this time, but the sky was beginning to clear up, as a strong westerly wind picked up.

In the coming days Ustad Ramzi remained bedridden, but he received clan members who came individually and in small groups to congratulate Ustad Ramzi on his resourcefulness. He sent them to see the cemetery and its newly whitewashed walls that the trainees had painted with a double coat of lime after the weather dried up. They also saw the bathed gravestones and the rose-stocks planted some days ago with the help of Banday Ali. The clan had collected a donation for laying a new pipeline that would eliminate the risk of future flooding.

Ustad Ramzi had not visited Gohar Jan for many days. He felt anxious and his nerves were strained, but his kneejoints had gotten worse. It was easier for him to move around with the help of a walking stick, but he experienced sudden spasms of pain. Walking more than a few steps was impossible for him.

Ustad Ramzi's condition deteriorated again when he contracted malarial fever. He was bedridden for a month and his diet was radically altered. Banday Ali visited him a few times during his illness, but Ustad Ramzi did not hear any news of Gohar Jan.

He slowly recovered, although his movements were still restricted.

STRIFE

Ustad Ramzi saw that the wild roses had made an appearance on one bough in the bushes planted in the cemetery. He smiled as he softly caressed the straight-petalled wild roses. Despite his careful pruning and the continuous grafting, one of its branches had escaped his notice. Nature's gentle strife had obviated his efforts.

In a spot from where a dead root had been removed, Ustad Ramzi planted another stock and sat down to make a few scions. The banyans and cypresses that lined the eastern boundary wall had extended their shade as the sun climbed up, and taken the edge off the hot gusts that had started circulating.

There were times when Ustad Ramzi thought about

the life he had given up: not with any feelings of regret, but with a desire to learn how, if at all, it might have changed him as a man. When reflecting on the choices he had made, and the existence he had bartered away, he often felt a curiosity about how life might have been different if he had chosen differently. There were many areas of his life in which these fancies at best remained incomplete pictures and half-realized emotions, and he increasingly felt that someone had lived inside him whom he had not fully recognized.

Sustained by a light diet in which milk had been replaced with water separated from curdled milk, his bodily powers had ebbed close to decrepitude. Now that his aggressive humours had quieted down and he no longer needed an outside influence to control them, Ustad Ramzi missed the evenings at Gohar Jan's kotha more than ever. He felt a desire to visit Gohar Jan's kotha and wondered why it was so.

Having ever held himself above succumbing to emotions, he was disturbed by the discovery of this longing in his heart. It put his own self-control and resolve in doubt and made him angry with himself.

In the same way that his careful grafting had still missed one rose bough, one association had brought to naught all his probity and care in the calibration of human relationships.

Once he ventured to Gohar Jan's kotha but, unable to climb the staircase for the pain, he returned.

He recalled the evening when he had visited Gohar Jan after Tamami's death. He had wanted to share his grief with someone, but his pride had not allowed the notion to take shape in his mind. He remembered that Gohar Jan only had sad reproach in her voice as she recalled her sister. Perhaps she pitied him for his inability to realize his own tragedy.

Ustad Ramzi no longer knew if it was grief he wanted to share or some guilt which he wished to confess to lighten his heart's burden before her.

PASSAGE

Some time passed. The bark on the trees became drier. In the kotha the sills of the windows and the lintels of the doors became loose. The steps on the stairwell splintered and broke; Banday Ali had to repair them himself.

Gohar Jan had survived a long bout of typhoid fever. She was convalescing when she received the notice from the municipality requiring them to vacate the premises within ninety days. The entire stretch of buildings was declared uninhabitable. Other kothas received similar notices.

Banday Ali asked Gohar Jan what she planned to do.

'We will find some other place,' she said.

'But what about seeking the mayor's help,' he reminded her. 'It is still not too late.'

'I have asked the last favour of him,' Gohar Jan replied.

Instead of arguing with her, Banday Ali went to see a lawyer of Gohar Jan's acquaintance to file an appeal on her behalf. The appeal was turned down, but the lawyer managed to get the court to grant a concession: an extension of ninety days in the final date to vacate the premises. Meanwhile, the residents had the option to demolish and rebuild.

When the builders came forward with their offer Gohar Jan accepted it, even though it was far lower than the property's value.

NEW RECKONINGS

Ustad Ramzi had requested Banday Ali's help in pruning the rose bushes. He sat close by and filled up small flowerpots with manure from a wheelbarrow. Their conversation drifted towards the deteriorating living conditions in the tawaifs' enclave where the water supply had been stopped. Apparently the water board had not been informed that the deadline for vacating the kothas had been extended. Acting on the earlier notice they had cut off the supply.

'I suspect it is the builders' doing. They may have bribed someone to ignore the new notice. Another trick to get us out of there sooner,' Banday Ali sighed as he pulled out a dead root. 'There's nobody to protest to.'

'But why didn't Gohar Jan call on the mayor to help her in the matter. It is common knowledge that the buildings are not as decrepit as they are made out to be. Surely the mayor could have helped her. At the minimum he could have ordered an inquiry and stayed the evacuation.'

'There is no arguing with Gohar Jan,' Banday Ali said. 'I can no longer even understand her. She told me she had asked the last favour of the mayor.'

Ustad Ramzi, who had not been able to solve the mystery behind the municipal help he had received, stopped in his work and looked at Banday Ali.

'At her age, too. To be without any anchor,' Banday Ali was saying. 'But this is life.'

Ustad Ramzi scrutinized Banday Ali's face again and realized he could not know about the last favour Gohar Jan had asked the mayor.

Ustad Ramzi was at a loss for words. He kept staring at Banday Ali.

'She never got any consolation from her art. Even though she remained true to it, giving up even her morning riyazat so that she could...' Banday Ali suddenly broke off.

'Gohar Jan gave up her morning riyazat?' a startled Ustad Ramzi asked. 'When?'

'She had given it up years ago.'

'Years ago?' Ustad Ramzi looked at him.

'It caused her too much effort to sing twice a day,' Banday Ali said after a brief silence. There was now a clear hint of a reproach in Banday Ali's voice. He returned to the pruning.

Ustad Ramzi knew of Gohar Jan's devotion to her art and the importance she attached to her morning riyazat. He wondered if what Banday Ali had implied was true.

Why did she do it? he asked himself. She could have ended her evening recitals instead.

He looked blankly at the peacocks strutting about among the rose bushes.

To hide his trembling hands, Ustad Ramzi vigorously broke the lumps of clay in the pot.

———

Ustad Ramzi began walking up to Gohar Jan's place every day. As he could no longer climb up, he sat at the foot of the stairwell where Banday Ali put out a chair for him.

'Ustad Ramzi is here,' Banday Ali would inform Gohar Jan when he arrived. Then Banday Ali would come down and join him.

They talked mostly about her condition.

The evacuation deadline was looming, but the exertion of moving things and her unspoken grief at the loss of her home caused Gohar Jan to relapse into illness and become bedridden. Ustad Ramzi learned this from Banday Ali when he came to see him a week before the deadline.

Her eyes had sunk into her face and she needed Banday Ali's support to move around the room. He cooked her light meals recommended by the doctor.

To make him happy Gohar Jan sometimes requested a special dish. On such days Banday Ali would be particularly restive, rushing into the kitchen every now and then to stir the food, adjust the heat, or add water or spices. He would decorate even the simple dishes of rice and lentils to make Gohar Jan feel that she was not on a convalescent's diet.

'Who would care for you if you fell ill?' she often said to him.

PASSING

It was a few hours to sunrise when there was a knock at Ustad Ramzi's door. He had not slept well. He found Banday Ali with the enclosure attendant. Banday Ali muttered an apology for disturbing him and said, 'Gohar Jan has passed away.'

'May God rest her soul,' Ustad Ramzi said softly. 'When did it happen?'

'About an hour ago. The evacuation deadline is tomorrow. Because I could not sleep I was making arrangements for the move when I heard her call out something. When I went into her room to enquire, she had already breathed her last. I must go back now to attend to the funeral arrangements.'

Around midday, when Ustad Ramzi arrived at the mosque, he was told that the funeral procession had left. Ustad Ramzi took a tonga and went to the municipal graveyard. Arriving there he found its gates closed. When he enquired from the flower-sellers at the gate they told him that only the funeral procession of an old man had come there that day. Ustad Ramzi reprimanded himself for not finding out the details from the mosque and for not visiting Gohar Jan's place first. He also felt angry with Banday Ali for delaying the burial in hot weather.

When he entered the tawaifs' enclave he heard that Banday Ali was searching for him. He found him outside the kotha. He had just returned after making a second trip to Ustad Ramzi's quarters in search of him.

'I have run into a problem,' Banday Ali said, looking troubled.

Thinking that he had run out of money, Ustad Ramzi took some money out from his pocket and asked, 'How much more is needed?'

'It's not a matter of money,' he told him.

Gohar Jan had a plot reserved in the municipal grave-yard. The gravedigger only needed to prepare it, and, early in the morning, Banday Ali had given him the in-structions. When he went to see if it was ready, the care-taker took him aside and told him that members of the funeral procession that had preceded Gohar Jan's had learned through his inadvertent remarks that the other grave he had dug close by was Gohar Jan's. Someone recognized the tawaif's name and immediately told the caretaker that they would not allow a prostitute to be buried with their kin. The caretaker had tried to reason with them, but he had stepped back when they threatened his safety. They filled up the newly dug grave, and a couple of them had stayed to keep an eye on things.

When Banday Ali arrived there, the caretaker regretted that he used Gohar Jan's own name. He told him the tawaifs were usually buried under assumed names for that purpose.

Returning in disappointment from the graveyard, Banday Ali thought of soliciting the help of Maulvi Yameen. He had agreed to say the funeral prayers, but he did not show up at the mosque as he had promised. At his house Banday Ali was told that he had to leave the city to deal with an emergency.

'The funeral prayer has not been said yet,' Banday Ali said. 'Gohar Jan did say once that in this world a tawaif's identity is the only one allowed to women like her. Yet she bestowed more dignity on these people than they are willing to claim for themselves. In her life she had provisioned for all eventualities. The only one she trusted to human charity was denied.'

Ustad Ramzi continued sitting long after the shovels were put away, and the trainees and few neighbours had left the cemetery in Ustad Ramzi's enclosure where all the graves had been filled.

When Gohar Jan's bier was brought there and Ustad Ramzi stepped forward to lead the funeral prayer, most of the trainees of his clan lined up behind him. A few men who had thronged the gates of the enclosure to watch the spectacle and gossip quickly cleared out at one look from him.

After the burial, Banday Ali pressed Ustad Ramzi's shoulder for a while quietly before taking his leave.

He was left alone in the cemetery.

He remained there in the growing silence, as darkness fell over the inner city.

ACKNOWLEDGEMENTS

For information about the pahalwans and the pahalwani culture, I am indebted to Akhtar Husain Sheikh's *Dastan-e Shehzoraan: Barre-Sagheer Pak wa Hind kay Namvar Pahalwanon ki Dastan – Vols I* and *II* (Lahore: Gora Publishers, 1995).

I am grateful to the Ontario Arts Council Writers' Work in Progress Grant which allowed me to devote time to work on the book. I would like to thank my publisher David Davidar, my editor Simar Puneet, my book designer Bena Sareen, photographer Sucheta Das, my agents Tom and Elaine Colchie, and my friend and mentor Robert B. Wyatt for all their help and support.

What is owed to my wife Michelle Farooqi's love and sacrifices cannot be put in words.